Baying the Moon

Learn to Howl, book 2

Jennifer R. Donohue

<u>Praise for Baying the Moon</u>

Baying the Moon is one of those rare sequels that equal and almost surpass the original book. I had so much fun reading it, and was turning the page nonstop, staying up all night, hooked and unable to put it down. So far, this is my favorite werewolf series of all time!

- Paul Jessup, author of The Skinless Man Counts to Five

• • • •

BAYING THE MOON PACKS heartbreak, humor, and gorgeous characters development into a fast-paced adventure as recent werewolf Allie and chaotic rocker werewolf Morgan contend with an evil pharmaceutical company and the complexities of family drama.

-Devan Barlow, author of the Curses & Curtains series

• • • •

DONOHUE DOES NOT DISAPPOINT in this exciting sequel to her werewolf story, Learn to Howl. As Allie copes with the revelations of the first book, the reader is right along with her in the emotional aftermath. The conflict around Silvernail was compelling, but the visceral feeling of loss and heartbreak really kept me turning pages even after the book was over. ~ Fiction Fans Podcast

• • • •

For Jim

• • • •

THIS IS A WORK OF FICTION. Names, characters, places, and incidents either

are the product of the author's imagination or are used fictitiously.

Any resemblance to actual persons, living or dead, events, or locales

is entirely coincidental.

No AI/LLM was used in the creation of this work.

Author Note

Hello and welcome to book 2 of the Learn to Howl trilogy, Baying the Moon. Thank you for continuing with me on this journey. When I first wrote Learn to Howl, I wasn't sure there was another book. I wrapped things up pretty well, right? Or well *enough*. But, in the way of things, I wasn't done spending time with these characters yet.

The werewolves in the Learn to Howl trilogy are different from typical movie werewolves; they are people and they are wolves, with no bipedal werewolf form in between. They're a little different from common pop culture urban fantasy werewolves; they're normal sized wolves, they don't communicate telepathically, and their social structures are more based on familial pack dynamics. I had a lot of fun with canine body language in the course of the trilogy, and maybe you will too!

Triggers for Baying the Moon include:
Medical experimentation
Threat of kidnapping
Gunshot injury
Miscarriage

Chapter One

Morgan's phone rang, and she made a face, and declined the call, all without swerving or seeming to actually much take her eyes off the road. I opened my mouth, and my phone rang. "Don't answer that," she said, dropping her phone in the drink holder. I dug my phone out and looked at the screen; it was Rachel.

"She'll murder me if I don't," I said.

"I doubt it." The phone stopped ringing.

"Did…did you tell her where we were going?" Something I should've asked hours ago, but Morgan seemed happy enough, singing along with her car tapes, and I kept my goody two shoes questions to myself and sang along too, when I knew the words. She'd had trouble with the clutch at a stop light not long after we got started and glared at me until she was sure I wasn't gonna ask if she was okay, then slid her sunglasses on. I could smell her pain. She was very good at ignoring me.

"I said we were going guitar shopping." Her dog Dio was in the back seat, tongue flagging in the wind. I'd thought he was a Catahoula, but apparently she bought him for twenty dollars from a box of puppies at a gas station. He'd hopped into the Jeep when he heard her keys, and she shrugged and got a jug of water to bring.

"Yeah, but did she know that meant you had a guy on the shore who like, sings guitars fully made from a magical grove of sycamore trees, and so it'd take a lot longer than, say, going two towns over?"

She thought about it for a minute, grinned. "Oh. No, I didn't. And anyway they're not sycamore. Maple maybe, or spruce. It depends."

My phone started ringing again. "We can't just keep ignoring her. She's gotta be really freaking out."

"We can just keep ignoring her."

"Are we really going guitar shopping?" Honestly, I'd decided I would believe her once we were in the music store parking lot. Fall and winter all cooped up, some of it laid up, and Morgan needed some kind of adventure to go off half-cocked on, before she killed us all.

She shrugged. "Well yeah. All mine burned up in the fire, except the partscaster in the back. Well and I think there's one in Vinnie's van."

"So did mine." Granted, I only ever had the one, battered and nameless acoustic thing that it had been even when it came into my possession, used to play songs at church on Sundays for God knows how long before I discovered I could find music I actually liked on the internet.

Morgan blinked at me. "Well aren't you just full of surprises. I didn't know you played too."

"You didn't ask," I said, still looking at my phone.

"We could've passed a lot of time screwing around with some guitars," she said. "Talking shop. Like, a whole winter where nobody let me *do* anything."

"Morgan you got *shot*, there's recovery time, for Heaven's sake. And besides, there's only so much I know. Probably none of it is anything you like," I said, and answered my phone. Even though I wasn't looking at her, it was like I could hear her rolling her eyes, and she heaved a sigh. At least she didn't hit me. "Hey Rachel."

"Alleluia," she said, and I almost laughed when she paused, just like Mama always would. It's tough to yell when you start out praising the Lord.

"I know we've been gone a long time, everything's fine," I said. "No shootouts, we're not in a ditch, nothing. We went to Morgan's P.O. box for her royalty check and she's gonna get a guitar and maybe we're gonna get a laptop so we can look at the stuff on the jump drive that the Wards gave me. You want us to bring anything back? Didn't Sidney say something about cookies? Oreos?"

"So you can...*what*?"

Morgan swerved to the shoulder abruptly, shoved the Jeep into neutral and yanked the emergency brake. A car blew past us, honking, and Dio barked at them. "Everything was so fucked up and confusing, I forgot that Everett gave me a jump drive with the stuff on it from that hard drives we pulled. And we can't exactly plug it into the wood stove. This is the first time you've let anybody leave since we got to, uh, where we've been. With the dogs and everybody." I didn't look at Morgan, but her stare just burned into me. I concentrated on Rachel, who was keeping her breathing even. It threw her off, I think, that I used the f word. On top of the rest of it.

"Just be careful," she said after what seemed like a very long time.

"I will," I said, relieved even though I knew it wasn't over yet. "We will."

"I believe *you* will," she said with a short bark of a laugh, and hung up.

"Jump drive?" Morgan asked, drawn out and deliberate, and I smiled apologetically.

"I found it in my jeans pocket this morning, it's a miracle I didn't wash them with the thing in it." The truth was typically pretty tame, except when it wasn't. "And like I said, we didn't have any computers and Rachel wasn't going to let us..." I trailed off, blinking away from her stare.

"Well." She let it hang there, in the thin spring sunlight, and then got back onto the road.

"You're not mad at me?" I looked out my window instead of at Morgan.

She took a real long time to answer me, but I kept from sneaking glances at her. Finally, she sighed. "Yeah, I am. Rachel is too. But it's cool, it's fine. We know now."

"I guess," I said. The tape, a Howling rough studio recording, stopped and clicked and turned over. I didn't know they still made cars with tape decks in them, but Morgan had assured me that, like vinyl, cassettes were making a comeback and she, for one, was thrilled.

"It's probably some kind of industry crime that it took me so long to even replace one guitar," she said as we shut the doors to her Jeep at the music store. A dog groomer's was next door, lots of neon signs in both the windows, and Dio hopped out and sniffed at that door with interest until Morgan snapped her fingers at him. "Don't tell anybody, they'll take my rock star license away." I'd never known what Morgan had in her room at the cabin; it could've been full of drugs or weapons or musical equipment, I'd never even cracked open the door. I didn't know why she'd have guitars in her room, if she was on tour with her band. Maybe they'd been in the Jeep when she was arrested, and Rachel carried them inside.

"Nobody'd believe me anyway." Her usual easy gait had a hitch in it that maybe only I would notice at this point, but between that and the driving, if I said anything about her hip bothering her, she'd probably kill me and drive that next few miles to dump my body into the ocean.

"Oh, they would. You've got that kind of face."

"Thanks." This was my first time that I'd been in a music store ever, but also in almost any kind of store since realizing my werewolf heritage that wasn't a gas station or rest stop, and the smell was a punch in the face. The wood and varnish of the instruments, the hot crackly scent of electronics, metal strings.

The guy behind the counter was tall and lanky, bearded and with kind eyes. He looked at us, looked at Morgan, and smiled. "It's been a long time," he said warmly. He held out his hand to Dio, who pushed in for ear scratches.

"Hey, Jerry," she said, also smiling. "Too long." Morgan never sounded more feral than when she was with people who were not wolves, and Jerry did not smell like a wolf.

"Business or pleasure?"

"Is there a difference?" She wandered to the array of acoustic guitars, some very plain and straightforward, pale lacquered and square-headstocked, like my old one, and some with elaborate pickguards and finishes.

Some kids came up to the register with packets of guitar strings, taking Jerry's attention. There were actually a lot of other people in the store, and I wasn't really sure what day it was. They'd all blurred together, and it hadn't mattered in a long time. There were mostly guitars, but some other instruments here too, an array of brass, a lonely drum kit, ukuleles and mandolins hung from the ceiling. Electric guitars too, which made it more surprising to me that Morgan had gone for the acoustics.

I wandered over to where she sat with a cobalt blue guitar in her lap, fiddling with the pegs, tuning it to itself. She had sort of a distant look in her eyes, and between that and her rare stillness, I just sat in another chair. Eventually she hit a few chords, then tapped out a rhythm on the uneven floorboards with the scuffed up toe of her boot. In a slower, lower voice than normal she sang one of her Howling songs, or one that was on a tape anyway. She'd at one point started to talk to me about doing covers, but either got frustrated with me or distracted by something else, I couldn't remember. Equally possible with Morgan. Especially when she thought I didn't know anything about music. Not that I knew how much I'd confidently say I knew about music.

"Planning an acoustic album?" I asked when she stopped. Morgan didn't really want me to tell her how good she sounded, how well she played. She already knew those things. The house where we stayed had electric, at least.

"Yeah, might be a thing to cash in on. Kind of do a solo thing from exile, just put it right on Bandcamp or something and horrify my agent. Well, the recording quality would be shit. The rest of Howling is guest starring with other bands right now. Or working fast food joints."

"You could. People do things like that all the time, don't they?"

"They do. Pity Rachel hasn't yet acknowledged the value and power of the information superhighway right?" She handed me the guitar and started browsing the rack again. "We could also drive down to Nashville, do a live press at a studio there."

"Rachel would definitely kill us. Hunt us down and kill us." She sighed a little, because it was such an Allie answer. Though really, it'd be a fun road trip. Driving around the country without a bunch of guns in the back, or waiting for somebody else to kidnap us, pick a fight, any number of things. Morgan picked enough fights all by her lonesome.

"Aw man, we should've had cameras and live streamed everything we did last year, we could've made bank. Viral found footage medical horror."

I shuddered. "I'm not sorry you didn't think of it until now."

Dio came and shouldered into Morgan's bad leg, and she flinched and did a short hard sniff through her nose and then scritched the top of his head. "Asshole." She looked at the guitar I held, my fingers poised reflexively on the neck. "You gonna play anything?"

"I don't know what to play." I looked away from her, glanced around the room, and laughed. "I know what not to play." There was a black sign on one wall that said NO STAIR-WAY.

"It'd figure that one's in your repertoire." Morgan shook her head.

"Non-church music wasn't exactly a facet of my household." That secret was my own, how long I was homeschooled before I fought bitterly enough that Mama let me go to high school. And then the kids at school were either into country, which I was not, metal, which I couldn't play, especially not on an acoustic guitar. Or. For once I was the one who smirked, though it was bittersweet, and I knocked out the opening bars of 'Sweet Home Alabama' while Morgan threw her head back and laughed.

"Glad you found a sense of humor someplace, anyway," she said. "You like that one?" She had another guitar in hand, all black, carvings I couldn't quite make out around the sound hole.

"I guess," I said.

"I think I like this one." She tinkered with it a bit, then without breaking eye contact did the opening riff of Dueling Banjos.

"Oh, now come on," I said. There were times I wondered that Rachel hadn't slapped my head off that first day, when I called our family hillbilly freaks. She raised an eyebrow. "No, Morgan."

"Well fine," she said with a sigh.

The other customers had thinned out and Jerry wandered over. "How many guitars could you possibly need?" he asked.

"Counterproductive, asking that in your line of work," she said easily. "I think I'll start with these two. I'll probably Craigslist a kicked-to-shit strat to mod up."

"You're killing me, Morgan," Jerry said, taking the guitar from me and pulling open a cabinet that was stacked with soft cases. "You know that multiple guitar companies come out with multiple new models every year? You're aware of this fact?"

"I know, I know, I'm sorry, but they're better when the new's worn off 'em." She didn't look very sorry. "And actually, give us the hard cases, Jerry. I like my guitar cases like I like my tacos."

"You stars are all such prima donnas," he said, and winked at me. "I guess we shouldn't be surprised, right?"

"Right," I said. "There's just no living with somebody like that."

Morgan dug out her wallet, and her bank card, and then poked around in the little containers of guitar picks but didn't get any. One of the guitar pick containers was full of Howling ones, and after that was when I noticed, too late to say anything without embarrassing myself, that there was a Howling poster on the wall, with a bunch of signatures on it in silver Sharpie, and then I saw the display of CDs. Just because I'd never heard of the band before coming to New Jersey didn't mean it couldn't've been popular. It really meant less than nothing, whether I'd heard of a band or not.

"You take care," she said to Jerry, and I realized they'd been carrying on while I was woolgathering, and then she picked up both guitars and shouldered out the door with Dio trotting happily next to her, so I was left to kind of awkwardly follow behind. I was always following behind Morgan, it seemed. Trying to keep up.

"Thanks for the guitar," I said once we were on the road again.

"Yeah, no problem. I feel mighty magnanimous when it's royalties time."

"I thought musicians didn't make all that much money." Maybe that was just something Mama told me when I made the mistake of starting to talk about taking an interest beyond hymns.

"Sometimes we do, sometimes we don't. We do good t-shirt sales, I guess, keychains, other merchandise shit. I dunno, I could read the statements but they're boring, I let the drummer do that. Vinnie. And the bitch at the label when we need to. So, what else do we need at Wal-Mart, since now we're getting a computer?"

"I...kind of thought I'd get some dog stuff. Well, wolf stuff." Rachel had promised to keep the wolf occupied while we were gone, but she'd thought we were taking a quick nearby run, not that we'd be gone for hours, or half the day. He had a big enclosure we'd made on the property, secure as we *could* make it, mostly me doing it under Rachel's watchful eye, metal posts, layers of wire, even a *lid* on the damn thing, but he still got bored and then got out. I'd been completely unprepared for the kind of management a real live wolf needed, of course. I spent a lot of time with him, I didn't have much else to do, but he wasn't a dog. He didn't want to hang out with me and play. He didn't want to take walks on the short leash that I had for him. He wanted to *run* and we didn't really have the tools for that. We couldn't just leave him loose like the dogs, because he was in no way inclined to stick close to people and cabin. So far we'd always been able to find him in time, but that luck wasn't going to hold.

She looked at me. "Stuff like what? A collar and matching bowls and a squeaky toys? You think that'll make him happy?"

"I thought I could take him in the woods on the harness and one of those steel tie-out cables. Maybe it'd work better than a normal short leash, and he'd try to get out less if he could do that."

"Yeah, maybe." I expected more, but Morgan just popped out the tape and stuck in another one.

Chapter Two

T he Wal-Mart parking lot was bigger than the store itself, and there was a line of RVs parked in the far end of it. Morgan regarded them with interest as we crossed the lot, and I imagined there must be a roving family of werewolves who traveled only in RVs. Nobody had mentioned it, but it made sense.

"Dio will be okay just in the Jeep?" I asked.

"There's no goddamn shade here, so we'll put the top up anyway. But it isn't hot enough and we won't take long."

"It feels really weird going to a store at all, after all this time. Much less a big one," I said.

Morgan shrugged and grabbed a cart. "I guess, but also I'll tell you a secret." I looked at her, eyebrows raised, and she smirked. "You know how people go visit the zoo? Sometimes I like to go visit a big box store. Or before all this, I could go into the city for the day."

"I keep forgetting you think of people as pitiful curiosities."

"Hey, why should I think I'm a freak? People are always so miserable. I'm comfortable in my skin." She looked at me for a long moment. "But lately *you* seem more comfortable in yours."

"Maybe more than I was a few months ago." Morgan's compliments were oblique enough, I didn't always notice them in time.

"Seven fucking months," she said, just a little too loud, and people in the early afternoon crowd moved away from us.

We went to look at the dog stuff first. There were a lot of the coiled steel tie-out cables, rubber coated, and Morgan tossed one in the cart. Would he want toys? Would he even know what to do with them, or would he just eat them? I didn't want to have to explain that to an emergency vet. If Rachel even let me take him to an emergency vet. "What else?" I asked.

"Really, we could probably all benefit from a whole lotta junk food." She did consider the toys for a minute, squeaked a couple of them, and then threw a non-squeaking rubber tire into the cart.

In the back corner of the store, there was a machine for engraving identification tags. I stopped and considered for a moment, and then picked a military dog tag shaped one for the wolf. As if he'd let anybody who wasn't one of us get near him if he got loose and far enough away. But just in case. Of course, to have a tag, your dog has to have a name. There hadn't been names on the cage in the Silvernail compound. I thought about it, and Morgan watched me. Then I laughed, because I got it, Morgan giving me the side eye for once instead of the other way around. What do you call an unidentified male? John Doe. I fed my money into the slot and Morgan read over my shoulder as I punched the buttons and she laughed too. On the back, I put "Allie" and the number for my most recent prepaid cell phone. The machine etched the tag in such a growling high pitch that I almost couldn't stand to be there, and when it was done I jammed the tag into my pocket, ears ringing.

Eyes watering, I trailed behind Morgan. I could smell the rotisserie chickens at the deli, and the fresh brownies in the bakery, the floor cleaning solution, and the brake fluid, and then we came to the electronics section. She stopped and looked around, and just spotted the laptops when we were interrupted by three boys in band t-shirts and ripped jeans at the other end of the aisle, elbowing each other and getting up the courage.

"Hey, are you the lead singer of Howling?" one of them asked. He couldn't look at her for very long, but was clearly the bravest of the group.

Morgan gave him her knife edge smile. "Why yes I am, thanks for asking."

"Oh, we've been to your concerts, we're big fans."

"Oh yeah? Where'd you see me?"

"The Saint, Dive, Starland," the tallest of them said. He had the beginnings of a goatee that he scratched at nervously. "Like, the albums are good but your shows are just amazing." I could just imagine Morgan on a stage with fans egging her on. Jesus help us.

I didn't know how I imagined her with fans, but she did have some level of grace anyway. "Well thanks. What can I do for you? You want autographs?"

"Yeah, if you don't mind. We knew better than to ask!" There was good natured, if slightly nervous, laughing all around at this. I wondered what Howling's shows were really like. Maybe she bit the heads off of things on stage.

They produced Sharpies, and Morgan signed notebooks, a wallet, and an arm. The one who got his arm signed was also the one who had been quietest, though after her name was temporarily immortalized in ink on his forearm, he admired it for a moment and said "I might go get this tattooed."

"Badass," Morgan said. "Tag us on Instagram, if you do it."

"Do you have any tattoos?" he asked after a moment of hesitation.

"Not yet." She grinned. "No piercings either."

"Hey, were you really at that place in Pennsylvania?"

Morgan glanced at me, our eyes meeting for a moment. "What place in Pennsylvania?"

"Some scientific place. I saw a news article that said you went all Patty Hearst at a research facility. Then I had to look up who Patty Hearst was."

Morgan thought a sec, head tilted, maybe also about who Patty Hearst was, then smirked. "Tell me, if you read an article that said Elvis went and shot up some random research facility, would you believe it?"

"Well. You're not dead."

"It's true, I'm not. I'm also not really a shoot 'em up kind of gal, right?" She had the scars on her knuckles to prove that, if they noticed.

"Yeah, I guess. I wasn't going to get another chance to ask though."

"You're right, I haven't exactly been active on social media lately. But hey, where was this article?"

"It was just a little weird news blurb on...actually where was it?" He looked at his friends, who shrugged.

"You know, never mind. I'll look it up when I go home, for a laugh. Is there a picture and everything? Gritty surveillance footage?"

"No, there wasn't a picture," the tall one said.

"I'm not sure if that's worse or better. Makes it seem far more made up."

"It makes a good story, I guess."

"So does running into the lead singer of Howling in a Wal-Mart. Here, let's do some selfies, and you can make all your friends jealous. You want some guitar picks? I've got guitar picks."

Eventually, the boys moved along, and Morgan's smile fell off as soon as they were out of sight. "I need to set up a god-damn Google alert for my name. Look, this laptop is less than three hundred bucks. USB ports and all."

"A Google alert won't do anything if we're always outside of service," I said.

A store employee approached us. He'd watched Morgan's interaction with her fans, I was pretty sure, and waited to see if we were going to steal something or be worth helping. "Can I help you with anything?"

"Yeah, what color do these come in?" Morgan jabbed her thumb at the laptop.

"They're silver or black. We also have decals if—"

"Gimme a black one. Do we need to pay for it here?"

"Yes. Though you can make all of your purchases at once, so you don't also need to go through checkout up front."

"Cool, thanks. While you're getting it out of the back, we're just going to grab a couple more things." She winked at him and walked off again to the toy aisle, which had an impressive selection of fake guns, small cowboy hats, and LEGO. "Oh hey, they sell handcuffs!" She held out one of the blister packs. I shook my head. "Oh, don't worry, they have a safety release on them. Though you have to wonder how many accidents there were before they implemented that particular feature."

"What kind of accidents could possibly be bad enough for them to still make toy metal handcuffs, but with a safety re-lease?"

"Oh, I don't know. Snidely Whiplash style getting tied to train tracks."

"I don't think that has to do with handcuffs." I wondered how she knew who Snidely Whiplash was, growing up in a house with no power in the Pine Barrens, but there was no way to tell what Morgan knew and how. Anyway, why would *I* know who Snidely Whiplash was, growing up homeschooled with no TV in a fringe fundie church my daddy made up?

"Maybe not. I'm sure they'll come in handy. And don't let me forget to tell you how to break a handcuffs chain with a seatbelt. Well, the metal click-in part of the seatbelt. What's that called, do you think? The tongue?"

"Why do....why would...You can do that?"

She laughed. "Yeah, you can do that. Saw it online." We loaded up the narrow electronics checkout shelf with assorted dog stuff, Oreos, and toy handcuffs. To his credit, the guy didn't bat an eye, just scanned and bagged. Even though she'd used a card at the guitar store, here Morgan paid cash from a derelict wad of tens and twenties she had in her jeans pocket, and we walked through the store with our receipt ready for the greeter to check over when he saw the laptop box.

"I didn't think anything like that would be in the news," I said to her once we cleared the automatic doors.

"I didn't either. Kind of a surprise, really. Unless they're fishing? They've gotta be fishing. I wonder what Bill Ward thinks of it."

"He's thrilled, I'm sure. His techs have turned in their report, fully compiled and with footnotes. They're sure to have all the Google alerts." We unloaded the cart into the back of the Jeep, Dio standing with his paws on the back of the seat to supervise.

"Don't tell Rachel we ran into groupies," she said abruptly.

"No? She isn't proud of her rock star daughter?"

She quirked her lips. "I'm sure she's proud in her own way."

"I don't like keeping things from Rachel," I said, shoving the cart into the nearby corral.

"I'm sure you don't. But it doesn't mean Rachel doesn't keep things from us either. The most recent example I can cite is a certain evil corporation by the name of Silvernail, and their unsavory extracurricular activities."

"Morgan, that doesn't make sense." When we'd shown Rachel the stolen book from the Wards, with the map and dates in the back of it that we figured was Silvernail activity, she'd taken the book, to read, while taking notes, but she hadn't said much to us and Morgan took that silence as a statement of guilt. I thought it was more like Rachel was furious at the Wards for sitting on that information. That intel.

"Turnabout is fair play. I've talked to fans before without being kidnapped any time after, by sinister corporations or otherwise. Gone on tour too. To other countries, even. Drop it." She lifted her lip a little.

"If you say so." I shrugged and looked out the window. I hadn't even really been arguing.

She let some time pass while I thought it over, I guess, and then said, "So, can I ask you something?"

I blinked. Morgan didn't ask to ask. "Um. Yes."

She didn't say anything right away, though, and it made me nervous. Finally, when I was ready to give up, she said "The boy in the woods. The football player."

It was my turn to not speak right away, as I wrestled with my stomach dropping, every muscle tensing. "What about him?"

"What do you want to do about him?" That hung between us for a second, as I waited to see if she'd say anything else, give me any guidance or just end up laughing about it in the Morgan way, but she didn't laugh. And I looked for the words.

"I don't know. And especially since everybody in town thinks I'm in Kenya on mission, I can't exactly make a late report now. And Mama wouldn't back me up. What's...what do people say?" I hadn't said much but I still felt breathless.

"Corroborate."

"Yeah. And I don't know what she told Daddy, or the boys." I tried to think, for a really long time, but I couldn't. I just heard my heart in my ears and thought about what coming to myself in the woods behind the house felt like. "I don't know," I said again.

"Think on it. You've started to come into your own with us, but I really feel like that's been, uh, a hellhound on your trail." She grinned slyly, and for once, I was the one who punched her in the shoulder.

"Did it take you this long to think of that joke?"

"Nah, I was just saving it for the right moment."

"Morgan. Thank you."

"Well, I didn't do anything yet," she said, like she wanted me to drop it, even though she was the one who brought it up. I just kind of wished that it was out of my hands, that some sort of cosmic justice would happen to that boy. Maybe that justice was Morgan.

Chapter Three

The Jeep lugged in low gear up the dirt road, and we finally topped off into the parking area in front of the cabin, Rachel and Sela sitting on the porch waiting, dogs lolling about around them in the afternoon sunshine. Dio poured himself out a back window and ran up onto the porch, nosed around like he was counting who was there, and then nose-pulled the screen door open and got himself inside.

"How is he?" I called.

"Laying on the floor in front of the fireplace, occasionally grunting. He doesn't care about any of the rest of us, you know. It's kind of funny."

"Funny because he doesn't much care about me either." I got the bags out of the backseat and pushed the door closed with my hip. Morgan had already installed herself on the porch, the guitars leaned up.

"What's that?" Sela asked.

"Laptop," Morgan said. "One of the Wards gave Allie Silvernail information on a jump drive before we left camp. We thought it was a good time to have a look."

"About time, I suppose," Rachel said. At a glance, I couldn't tell if she was mad I'd sat on that information for so long. I really hadn't left the jump drive in my jeans for so long, I'd put it in a drawer in my room, buried in clothes. But I knew Morgan wasn't in any condition to act on anything we found out, and I knew what we found out would be upsetting, if what little Everett told me was any indication.

"For what?" Sidney asked, coming out onto the porch. She was always already supporting her belly with one or both hands as she walked around, and I wondered if she was fixing to have twins. "Oh wow, are those red velvet?"

"They sure are," I said, tossing her the package. Sidney seemed to be the only one of us who still liked chocolate. There wasn't any chocolate at any of the Ward locations, that I remembered. Vanilla protein powder, never chocolate.

"Give me the thinger," Morgan said, and I handed the drive over.

"Everett said he didn't organize the files or anything, just pulled them off the Silvernail hard drives you got."

"Which one was Everett again?" Rachel asked.

"The skinnier one with spiked hair," I said after a moment's consideration. "The taller one who was on our team when we got you out." She just nodded.

"Well, there's a lot of stuff here, and things like 'Subject A' instead of names. I doubt they knew anybody's names."

"Hard to say," Sela said quietly. She'd gotten very still and small, since the laptop came out. "They never said anything to me, just talked around me."

"Oh, they talked to me," Rachel said. "They tried to see just how much they could piss me off, and what I'd do about it. I guess they've seen too many movies where critters get angry and Hulk out." She thought for a second. "No names, though."

"Too bad we didn't think to get a printer too," Morgan said. I looked over her shoulder; the file she was scrolling through had lots of charts. "Staring at screens for too long gives me a headache. I can see the flicker." Maybe it was why she used a flip phone, too.

"How many files are there?" I asked. I had to look away after a couple minutes; I could see the flicker too. I didn't used to.

"A whole bunch. Hundreds. They're labeled things like endocrinology, Subjects A, B et cetera, heritability, and silver. And a lot of unreadable shit that's raw data or needs a special program to open or something, I dunno."

I seized on the detail I could make the most sense of. I didn't used to always be this easily overwhelmed, either. "Just silver?"

"Yeah, just silver." Morgan opened that one and started scanning it, squinting. A muscle in her jaw twitched. "They seem to think silver affects us the way radioactive things would. Like, it has to do with proximity, purity, and duration of exposure."

I looked at the scar on my thumb, from where I was wearing a silver spoon ring the first time I changed. "It doesn't not make sense, anyway."

"Yup." Morgan closed the laptop. "I'm going to take this thing inside and plug it in. I copied the files to it already, so you can have the thinger back. Maybe bury it in a coffee can, so we have it as backup."

"Jump drive. Flash drive. Memory stick." I couldn't help it, but she laughed; of course she was trying to get a rise.

"Whatever. The world's already moved on to cloud computing." The screen door slammed behind her. Sidney, crunching another cookie, followed her. It hadn't occurred to me that Sidney might be jonesing for some computer time, after coming from the modern world back to this. At least the cabin had electric.

"If they compiled that much information from us in just a few days, imagine what the Wards must have skimmed off them by now from that virus they put on the server," Rachel said.

"You think it's time to make contact?" Sela asked.

"I think it might be time, yeah. Past time. We're all healed up, more or less," She glanced at the door. "And we don't need Ward drawing undue attention if he gets antsy and can't find us."

"It's a shame it was the Wards," Sela said.

"It is what it is," Rachel said. She got up and went inside as well.

I looked at Sela. "The Wards did okay by us, more or less. What they pulled at the end there wasn't so great." And at the beginning, when they gave us the runaround and Morgan started that fight. Maybe the Wards didn't actually do okay by us. I'm sure Morgan was looking forward to fighting Luke more, no further reasons necessary.

"They did. But those men aren't satisfied if they're not the ones running things. They're good allies to have, but I don't assume for one minute they're our friends."

"Who are our friends? Do we have any?"

Sela gave me a tired smile. "Sweetie, I'm sorry, I think we forgot you were still totally new to all this. Then it was you and Morgan and—" she laughed and shook her head. "Anyway, The Coutards can be trusted to be neutral about family disputes, absolutely. They'll always send a mediator, when asked. Maybe they'd do more, and by "they" I mostly mean Ardith because her sister Hunter is a little more like our Morgan. There are some cousins, I guess. But nobody's had an outside threat like this before, least not modernly and with that level of resources. Let's see...the Nortons could be considered friends, yes."

I waited, but she didn't go on. I didn't know who the Nortons were. Sela and Rachel must not have known that Morgan called Hunter Coutard for help, or information anyway, while we were looking for them. "That's it?"

"That's about it. Oh, there are more families, but we all keep to ourselves and tend our own backyards. Go to the Coutard meetups when they happen and posture and shake hands on neutral ground. It doesn't mean everybody's hostile, mind you, it's nice to be around wolves and not have to be constantly pretending. It's just every family is different, has different ways. We run into each other once in a while, outside of that, maybe talk a little, maybe not."

"Depends on if moonshine is available?"

"Actually, that's a funny one for you. That moonshine? It's always Culver moonshine."

"Really?" I smiled.

"Yeah, really. We've been making it the longest, with the same recipe. I guess during Prohibition, we were the ones who outlasted ATF suspicion, if it fell on us at all. We were never raided."

"Interesting." I thought of how many generations ago Prohibition was for us. Our shortened lifespan made it hard; I thought maybe Amity Culver would've been the family matriarch during the twenties and thirties. I'd check the family Bible later, to see.

But I'd put it off long enough, and went inside to see the wolf. The newly christened John Doe. He was actually pretty good, somehow, so far as household pet standards were concerned. He didn't care about any of us, and mostly spent his time avoiding us. Even the dogs, and *that* was a relief. He seemed to like being in the enclosure, if I could say that he liked anything, though I tended to have him in my room at night. If he got away in the overnight, we'd never find him, and he'd get shot by police or by somebody protecting their land, and he was the wrong kind of wolf for the area. Well. There weren't supposed to be any wolves in the area. That was sure to lead to questions we didn't want, people poking around where we didn't want.

The wolf raised his head when I came into the cabin. I got his harness off a hook by the door, and came over to him, steel line in my hands. I looked down at him, and he looked up into my eyes, questioning, but I wasn't really sure what he was asking. People talk of these profound encounters that they have with wildlife, these magic moments when their gazes meet and they gain an understanding of the animal they're facing. Maybe they were just better at it than I was. Or maybe they were lying. I held out my open hand to him, and he sniffed it delicately. After a moment, he swiped my thumb with his tongue. He let me put the harness on him without any struggle, but he never showed any joy to me, or excitement. He seemed to be healthy enough, but I didn't know what else those people did to him. It just didn't seem like normal wolf behavior, for him to be so unresisting. Maybe Silvernail had him for long enough that he didn't know how he was supposed to act. I fastened the line to the wolf's harness, and then ran it around my waist and closed it with a carabiner.

"Be careful now," Sela said. She was already coming in to get dinner ready.

"I will." I looked at Morgan, lounged across one of the couches, boots still on. "You wanna come for a run?" Maybe I'd kind of already had enough Morgan time for today, but I couldn't not offer.

"Nah," she said, with a jaw cracking yawn. "I'm gonna screw around with this for a little while, but really, we need to call Fran for this doctor shit. So maybe I'll screw around with some song writing, and then it'll be dinner and bedtime. It's like we're some kind of fucked up farmers."

"Language," Sela said from the kitchen.

"Ma'am," Morgan said, but in the exact same tone of voice, not apologetically.

Outside, I lifted my face to the wind and inhaled the scents. The cooling engine of the Jeep, Rachel's recently constructed moonshine still even though apparently it wasn't the right season for it. According to Morgan. The woods were lovely. Different from the Pine Barrens. Older, darker, the soil far loamier. There were a lot more squirrels here, but I didn't guess that would last very long, with all the dogs. And the wolf. He'd caught enough squirrels that I'd lost count already.

He wandered and I followed him, leash walking not really something either of us knew about, and I thought about Kyle. Or, what I would want done about Kyle. I didn't want to sit in the Sheriff's office and tell him, and whoever else needed to hear what happened, over and over again. Because to me, nothing *really* happened, and I wouldn't be able to truthfully tell them how I stopped him. It was something I wanted to forget; I could understand why some people, when they were attacked, just went home and showered and tried to get on with their lives. And I could understand why some people fought as hard and publicly as they could. But I didn't want him to hurt anybody else. He probably already had, but I didn't want him to hurt anybody else because I just ran away. I'd feel like it was my fault, whether that was true or not.

But what Morgan was asking me, she didn't mean for that to be public, or legal, I didn't think. Morgan was the only one I knew without a shadow of a doubt had killed people on our Silvernail raids. And she was the one who had escalated with the Wards, to get them to listen to us. I got the feeling that if I wanted her to drive down to Alabama and perform some very specific violence on Kyle Dodd, she would, and it was terrifying and comforting at the same time, and I didn't know how such a thing was possible.

Chapter Four

The next morning, Morgan woke me up by leaning over me and singing "Who's Afraid of the Big Bad Wolf?" I jerked upright, and almost head-butted her, but she dodged out of the way, laughing.

"Is he out again? What happened?"

"What? No, he's on the floor there." She pointed, and the wolf was curled up on the floor in the corner, head still on his paws, yellow eyes fixed on me. "It's breakfast time, and on top of that, Rachel's ready to go call the Wards and wants us along."

"Well alright," I said, even though Morgan was already out the door again, thumping down the stairs. Sausage and biscuits for breakfast, by the smell of it. Getting to go out two days in a row, that was really something. Rachel must've been getting as stir crazy...well, as me. I was sure nobody was as stir crazy as Morgan except maybe for John Doe. A thing I knew now that I didn't before was that Morgan didn't really sleep, not like the rest of us; she was up any hour of the night, and often out of the house before any of the rest of us woke up, coming back smelling like woods and wolfchange.

At least Morgan didn't eat rocking chairs, or hadn't yet.

"Where are you going?" Sidney asked as I came into the kitchen and poured myself a cup of coffee.

"To where we can get service, to call the Wards."

"Oh. Time to get this show on the road, huh?"

"Morgan seems to think so," I said. Mouth full, Morgan shook her head and stuck her empty plate in the sink before stalking off, limp pronounced. It seemed worse in the mornings, to me anyway. Whether she'd gone out running or not. We both watched her go for a moment. "Rachel too."

"A year ago I might've thought so too." She quirked her lips and looked down at her baby belly. "Right now, though, I'd prefer to be invisible. Mama too, I know."

"Well, there's only so much room in the car," I said with a smile. "Babies are important, Sidney. Don't feel bad."

"I don't, most of the time. Morgan just has that way about her."

"I think of it as wolfier-than-thou."

Sidney threw her head back and laughed. "Oh, that's good. I'll remember that."

"Just remember to give credit where credit is due."

"Of course." A horn squawked out front, just barely. "I guess I'll see you later," Sidney said.

"Yeah, see you. You want me to put him in the enclosure?"

"No, I'll sit and read, and he'll spend his time ignoring me. It's a thing we do."

"All right." Maybe we should've gotten her some books, when we were out the other day. She probably read all the ones here. The horn honked again. "Bye."

We took Rachel's beat up black Bronco and didn't talk on the ride into town. There was a general store with a payphone on the side of it, and when Rachel parked, she and Morgan went in opposite directions and checked around first for people before Rachel dialed. I stood out front and took in the scene. So much for needing cell service. The general store had old fashioned gas pumps in front of it, the chrome and glass types. If you had a credit card, you had to go inside. Maybe a couple of good old boys with glass bottled cokes would normally be installed in the rocking chairs on the front porch, but not just now.

I watched Rachel as she dropped her quarters and the call rang through. Morgan sat on the hood of the Bronco and looked around. "Hey Bill, it's Rachel. Yeah, I thought it was about time you shared what information you got online." She smiled just a little, glancing over at Morgan and I. "Well, no, I'm not going to do that. How about we pick some neutral ground to meet on?" She listened again. "Well that sounds just fine. I take that to mean you're no longer at your usual, what is it, Alpha base?" She grinned and looked just like Morgan for that instant. "Yeah, two days. Sounds good. Bye now."

"He actually thought you'd tell him where we were?" I asked.

"He actually did. He was inclined to be growly about it. Bill seems as though he feels pretty proprietary over our attention."

"New York isn't where any of us live," Morgan said, I thought for my benefit. She was standing close enough to hear Bill on the phone "Ardith and Hunter live in Pennsylvania."

Rachel smiled again, her head tilted just a little. "Funny you mention the Coutards. Do you think Bill is on the phone with Ardith right now, asking for a mediator?"

"He's probably got a file on them too. Intel." Morgan made exaggerated air quotes and Rachel snorts.

"He's got files on everybody. There are worse ways to run things, I guess; it just isn't ours."

Morgan shrugged. "Bill Ward just gets my back up."

"You sure handle the Wards well enough," I said, mostly to keep from feeling left out.

"Well thanks, cuz. It's all about knowing what they respect, right?" She winked at me.

"Right, strength and balls." I rolled my eyes.

"What's this?" Rachel asked, still smiling a bit, but watching us. It was funny, having a secret from Rachel. She never intended Morgan to be my werewolf mentor, but it happened anyway.

"Aw, didn't we tell you?"

Rachel sniffed. "No, Morgan, you did not. You'd best get to it soon."

"We're talking about what we did to get the Wards on board. We went to some gentleman's club they frequent, The Bear's Den. Once inside, we were promptly thrown out for being *girls*. So I got the tire iron and gave Allie the bat, and I broke the rear windshield of Bill Ward's pickup. He's got vanity plates, you know, they say Alpha."

"You what?" Rachel's eyes narrowed.

"Well, the alarm went off of course, the thing was flashing and beeping, and what was it, four, five Wards came out?" Morgan glanced at me and I nodded. "I broke the nose on one, stomped another's knee, wrenched an elbow, and then Bill called them off."

"What did Allie do?" Rachel asked. She seemed amused and angry at the same time. Funny that Morgan kept me from telling Sela this very story, much earlier in our adventure.

"In the parking lot? Not a damn thing. Inside, though, she insulted their manhood until they agreed to help us."

Rachel turned to me and fixed me with those icy blue Culver eyes. "How true is this, Alleluia?"

"Well, while Morgan is being kinder to me than I thought she would, it's all true. The bouncer kicked us out, Morgan got that stuff out the back of the Jeep, I realized a little too late what she was doing, and there we were."

"Yeah, but what did you say?"

"I said that if they couldn't be bothered, even though it was sure to be their necks as well soon enough, I'd find somebody who could. I asked who was more important."

"I wish we'd gotten you sooner," Rachel said ruefully. "By the time I was able to think, I was so glad that I sent you off to pick up Morgan. I didn't know what you would do, but I figured Morgan would find a way. I'm proud of both of you."

"Aw, Rachel, getting emotional in the parking lot? We're all going soft," Morgan said. "Should we hug too? I feel a hug coming on."

"Sweetheart, you can have a hug whenever you want," Rachel said, honey-toned, and grabbed Morgan before I even keyed in to the fact that she meant to move. I saw Morgan twitch to get away, but Rachel was faster. I couldn't decide if the moment was touching, or hilarious. Both.

Morgan froze and put up with it well enough at first, and then started to wriggle. "Come on now, Rachel."

Rachel let go, but not after holding on just another couple seconds longer. "I kinda like it better when you call me Mama."

"I know, but I've only got so many of them in me. You already got one last year, I've gotta save this year's for Christmas."

"Yes, daughter mine, unable to take a knife to her mother's flesh."

"Much as I love walking down memory lane, don't you think we should be moving along?" I asked. Morgan's eyes flashed to mine, grateful. For all her bravado, I could still hear her voice when Rachel told her to cut out the microchip that the Silvernail experimenters had implanted in her shoulder blade: *Mama, I can't.* Those were my contributions: browbeat Bill Ward into giving us his support, shot some drones, and dug a microchip out of Rachel's shoulder. As it turned out, it had been enough.

"Do we need anything while we're out?"

"I didn't check the fridge," Morgan muttered.

"So other than the Coutards, who are apparently werewolf Switzerland, is there a family everybody thinks is important? I mean, the Wards think they're great because they're all commando, but is there consensus? Is it just the Coutards?"

"What, you asking if we have a werewolf royal family?" Morgan could not make it more clear she thought my question was stupid.

"Not exactly. I don't know." I shrugged.

"We just don't work like that, Allie," Rachel said. "For safety, we live separate. We crave the companionship of other wolves, except when we hate it. We want to live in the family unit, and we're suspicious of outsiders. And normal humans are so much like sheep."

"Excepting we don't hunt them," I said.

"Not normally."

"But sometimes?"

Morgan turned around to look at me. "What exactly do you think any of our plans here are going to involve?" she asked me, like *I* was the unreasonable one.

Chapter Five

T he motel had its own bar. It wasn't really *in* New York either; we couldn't even see the city skyline, though we'd driven ever-closer to it before the highway winged us past. The Alpha pickup truck was already there, with its impressive array of antennae, rear windshield replaced. There were shotguns in the rear rack. After we'd passed it and as Rachel knocked on the room door the truck was parked in front of, I realized that I smelled more than Bill. Luke, but that was to be expected, but also Joe and Everett, which was not. A red haired woman with light brown eyes opened the door, and I'd never been able to say I could smell disappointment before, but Morgan smelled disappointed. "Rachel," the woman said with a smile.

"Ardith, I'm glad you could make it."

"Culvers and Wards working together is momentous. I'm a little surprised you didn't call me a few months back."

"They went and found the Wards instead." So Hunter hadn't talked about Morgan's call. Calls.

Ardith nodded, her eyes darting over Morgan, and resting on me for a moment. "A shame. Well, I'm here now."

We stepped inside. There were a couple of laptops in bags on one of the beds, and Everett and Joe sat on the other one, watching television. "I have to say, Bill, I wasn't expecting quite this group," Rachel said, an edge in her voice.

"You brought yours, I brought mine." Bill stared at each of us for just a little too long. "Besides having called Coutard."

"I agree, a mediator isn't a bad idea," Rachel said smoothly. "You know the trouble our tempers could get us in."

"It's a shame we can't just work together peacefully," Bill said, in that way that got my back up, like us *ladies* were always so unreasonable.

"Sure is. We'll manage somehow." Yelling on the television screen drew my eyes; it seemed like the weather channel, and people were driving at a tornado.

"Cut to the chase, Bill, what did you find out? What were they after?"

"Remember how you laughed at me and told me that the government didn't want super soldiers, that one time?" Rachel actually rolled her eyes, but then she nodded. "Well, the government wants super soldiers. Among other things."

"Seems like they overestimated our abilities," Rachel said dryly.

"That may be. But once the gene for something is isolated, that gene can always get put into overdrive. So Everett tells me, from the computer work he's done." Everett turned around when he heard his name, and our eyes met briefly before he turned to Bill.

"Yeah, we got a lot of intel when everybody tried to sign into the server the next day. It's funny, you'd think those scientist types would be a lot smarter than that. Or maybe they didn't get the word out fast enough, it's hard to say."

"Or they fed you fake information," Rachel said.

"Well yeah, that's possible, but they'd've had to fill up a bunch of peoples' home machines ahead of time with all this fake stuff. I'm not saying they couldn't have, but with how cocky they were? Not likely."

"All right then. I assume you brought copies of this for us?"

Bill nodded to the laptops. "It's on there, but I'm not sure where you get away thinking we're just going to hand stuff over, especially after you walked away from us like that."

"Way I see it, Bill, most of that is mine outright. I bled for it, my daughter bled for it, my sister died for it. Some of that is medical records that they formed on me, and on my sisters. That isn't anything you've got any right to claim, in anybody's way of thinking."

"Our resources got you out of there." Luke spoke for the first time, and he was looking at Morgan.

"Oh, this again," Rachel said, raising her eyes to the ceiling.

"Your resources got us to the door. I got her out of there," Morgan said, baring her teeth. I couldn't say reliably whether her hands were fists already, or if she made them just for Luke. "Me and Allie. You never opened the door for us, and Joe and Everett backed that story up."

Ardith raised her hands and stepped in between where everybody stood off. "I'll tell you what, how about we grownups go to the lounge, and we have some whiskey over this, if they have whiskey, and talk it out a little bit."

"Grownups?" Morgan flashed, and Rachel gave her a warning glare.

"The over twenty-fives? Does that work better for you?" Ardith smiled mildly. She looked older than Morgan and younger than the aunts. I looked from her to Morgan, and noticed Luke also looking at Morgan. "I don't want to make light of the roles that anybody plays here, but the people going to the bar are me and Rachel and Luke and Bill."

"Sure, yeah," Morgan muttered.

Rachel half-sighed. "Nobody else seems to mind, I'm sure you can pass the time for a little while." The boys looked a little like they'd each swallowed a frog. I was glad that I wouldn't have to just be hanging out in a little hotel room with Luke Ward.

"Of course we'll be fine," I said, looking at another tornado on screen, or maybe the same one. I sat on the edge of the bed with the laptops, and Joe hopped to his feet and picked them up, moving them to the floor against the wall.

Bill made an 'eyes on you' gesture at the boys. "Behave," he said, staring at each of them in turn. Luke seemed amused, and Rachel did too, but I was sure it was for different reasons.

"We will, sir," the boys said, and the grownups made their departure to the bar. I assumed whiskey was taking the place of moonshine as a good faith gesture.

"We don't have to watch this," Joe said, smiling. He'd always been the easiest to get along with, of the Wards. "You can choose, if that helps ease things at all."

Morgan looked at him a moment, and then laughed. "In a way, storm chasing is what we're doing, isn't it?" She sprawled out across the double bed I was sitting on, her boots hanging off the side. She had her prepaid out, and was texting, probably Hunter. I didn't know if she tended to text people other than Hunter, actually. Her band, maybe? I craned my neck to try and see, but she stuck her tongue out at me and rolled away onto her back, phone in front of her face. We were on to the local forecasts when Morgan said, "So did you guys miss us? How have you been passing the time?"

"Did my ASVAB" Everett said, after a pause, probably wondering if she actually cared or not.

"Oh yeah? That eager to join up?"

Everett shrugged. "It's what we do. And I'd be in like, coding or drone operation or whatever. I don't want to be a SEAL like Luke was."

"Luke's a SEAL?" she asked. "*Was* a SEAL?"

"Yeah he's out now," Joe said, looking at me for help that I honestly didn't know how to give him. Heaven help us if Morgan latched onto that too hard.

"And came right home to run ops in Bill's shadow, isn't that something. You boys're lucky we came alone then, huh? To actually give him an op? They should be thanking us." She elbowed me.

"Yeah," I said, and she made a face at me. I guessed it seemed like I lacked conviction. "Like enriching his enclosure," I said, and was surprised at how hard it made Morgan laugh. Joe did too though.

"Maybe you're right," he said. "Thank you."

"Our pleasure," Morgan said, and then her phone buzzed again and she went back to it. I could only imagine that some of her late night ramblings were to a place with signal enough that she could text Hunter; seven months was a long time to not see your girlfriend, especially if you were hurt.

After an hour, even Everett got antsy. "So hey, how long you figure they're going to be?" he asked, looking at the door. Not so much of a Howling fan that he was taking the time to be star struck this time. He hadn't asked for Morgan's autograph either. He couldn't really take one back to any Ward household and live it down.

"Yeah, who can say," Morgan said, not looking up. "Not one of us likes getting pushed around. But we'll definitely know pretty quick if they start throwing punches."

"I haven't seen Grandpa fight anybody in years," Joe said uneasily.

"Well and I haven't seen him fight anybody ever, so I really missed out, huh?" We all laughed at that. "So they're not gonna have plans that include us, not really," Morgan said.

"No, probably not much more than this," Everett said. I wished he sounded more cautious; he'd seen Morgan in action, he couldn't expect anything good would come of that line of thinking. Or maybe he was eager for more action before getting recruited to whichever branch he ended up going with. Joe and I exchanged a look.

"And you've got all the intel anyway. So maybe you can load some more of it on the—"

"Jump drive," I said, before she could call it something else weird. No sense asking how she knew I brought it, she smelled it. I got it out of my pocket and tossed it to Everett.

"Just so we have it, you understand."

"Yeah, no problem," he said.

Joe said, "And then we should—"

"Wait to see what they say," Everett interrupted, plugging the jump drive in on the first try.

"Don't hurt to have a backup plan," Joe muttered.

Another hour and Rachel came back, followed closely by the others. I couldn't really read Rachel's expression, just her tension, and Morgan tensed up next to me. Nobody was drunk, but I could smell the whiskey. Ardith was the only one who still seemed as relaxed as when everybody had first arrived.

"We'll have all the data we want," Rachel said.

"But?" I asked, my thoughts trying to run wild and not coming up with anything at all.

"But we're bringing Joe and Everett with us for a visit."

"Oh, well is that all?" Morgan sniffed and looked at them. "I guess you boys are happy about that."

"It depends," Everett said gamely, and at the same time Joe said "That could be fun."

"We don't have internet."

"Then no, not really," Everett admitted, and Luke laughed, short and ugly.

"I'm sure you'll find something to do," Bill said. "They still have electricity, I assume."

"Running water, too," Rachel said dryly. The house in the Pine Barrens didn't have those things, but Bill didn't need to know that if he didn't already.

"Well thank God for that."

"This isn't a trade, is it?" I asked, a thought finally breaking free. I hoped not, I really hoped not. I didn't think so, but I hoped not.

"Nah, we're not shipping you off to the Ward camp. They're just sending those two along with us since they have so many extras. Everett has all of the information from the hard drives and that the virus skimmed on both of those laptops, and he's their youngest computer whiz. Maybe it'll be good for you girls to learn something."

"I think we both know how to use computers, Rachel." Morgan glanced at me, just long enough to make sure I wasn't going to tell on us.

"Well, it's too much information to cover in an afternoon while knocking back Jack Daniels, so that's another reason."

"I agree with Joe, it could be fun," I said, and when Bill looked at me I smiled sweetly. I could play the game, for a little while at least. At least it wasn't Luke and Bill wanting to come up to the cabin, with Sidney pregnant, and me constantly trying to deal with the wolf. Maybe Joe would be happy to get away from Luke for a while, I could more than understand that. Mostly everybody seemed to treat Joe right, but the mean ones were sure to do it when Bill wasn't around.

"All right then," Ardith said. "I believe I'll look in on you after a time, make sure everybody's getting along, and to learn what you've found out. Acceptable?"

"Yes, it is," Rachel said with a smile. "Maybe bring Hunter when you do. I'm surprised you didn't this time. Thanks for coming out."

"Oh, you know how she is about politics," Ardith said, smiling when Morgan frowned. She hugged Rachel, and shook hands with the men before heading out the door.

Rachel turned to the Wards. "Well, boys, we'd like to hit the road, so get your bags and say your goodbyes. Bill, we'll be in touch."

"How can I reach you?" Bill asked. It rankled, that Ardith knew where we were but he wouldn't.

Rachel smiled. "We'll check in every week or so. Not to worry, though, they're in good hands."

Chapter Six

The ride back to the cabin was quiet, though not as tense as I'd expected. Morgan put in a non-Howling tape, a surprise that I didn't comment on. Joe took the other window seat, leaned his head back, and promptly dozed off. Everett sat in between us and played some shooting game on his tablet for most of the drive. Rachel didn't take the same way back that she did to New York; this was certainly the scenic route, and it was getting on dusk when we pulled up the drive to the cabin.

Sela and Sidney came out on the porch. The wolf's enclosure was behind the cabin, so I couldn't see it, but I saw the look on Sidney's face and put my nose to the wind and knew he wasn't there. I ran up the porch steps to her. "What happened?" I asked in a low voice.

"Well, after a while, I put him in the enclosure. He seemed like he was settled in and being relaxed, but what he was really doing was digging one of the posts loose. I can't run like this," she said, teary-eyed.

"It's not like he hasn't done this before, Sidney, and I really didn't expect you to chase after him if this happened. I just hoped that the wire at the bottom would be good enough." I guess we should've added sheet metal.

Morgan came up behind me. "Again?" she asked.

"Yeah. I'll go out the back."

"Have a nice run," she said, punching me in the shoulder.

"Yeah, thanks. Have fun getting Joe and Everett acclimated. Maybe they'll want to play pinochle."

"Or strip poker."

Oh boy. "Count me out."

"Like you need to tell me," she said, rolling her eyes and turning back to Rachel.

I went through the cabin, picking up the coiled steel tie out cable along the way. Other than when he was still on sedation and God knew what other drugs in the Silvernail compound, he had never bared a tooth at me, and I wasn't really worried about what would happen when I found him, only worried that I'd find him before he got into trouble. I passed through the kitchen and gave dinner on the stove a cursory sniff; it was a big pot of chili, and the cornbread in the oven was almost done. When I went into the woods behind the cabin, head and nose down for the wolf's trail, I heard Joe ask "Where did Allie go?"

I paused, just under the pines, and heard Morgan gruffly say "You don't need to worry about that," and then Sela picked up the patter, talking about how tired they must be after all that driving around, and scolding herself for not having dinner ready and on the table for the guests. It occurred to me that the pot of chili was more than would normally just get cooked for the group of us; I guess the aunts had anticipated something like this happening. Maybe I was the only one who didn't.

At first, the wolf made a straight line away from the enclosure. After that, it looked like he took off after a squirrel or a rabbit, and then it got away. From there, he roamed in a big circle, and I wondered what he was looking for. Maybe he was just getting the lay of the land; in about ten minutes, I reached the property line, with the blaze orange POSTED and NO TRESPASSING signs, and of course the wolf's trail went right past them and into the national forest next door.

I didn't know how many more times I could do this, track him down and get him back to the cabin. Every other time, I'd caught up with him on a different part of the property, but still on our property, and having escaped outside notice. My chances of that were dropping with every step I took, and I stopped and closed my eyes, raising my face to the slight breeze that came through. I inhaled slowly, carefully. He was still pretty close, but so were people. Crap. I'd never tried to go both as fast as I could and as quietly as I could at the same time, in the woods, but there's a first time for everything. I didn't fool myself that he wouldn't hear me coming.

The trees thinned out even more, and I was starting to smell parking lot, and road, and cars in the distance. I slowed my jog and took more care, scanning the forest around me. My eyes caught on a glint of metal, and I realized it was the John Doe tag that I'd made. So he hadn't slipped his collar, and I thanked God for small favors. I crept in, and then looked where he was looking. There were three or four people standing around smoking and talking, maybe hikers. Or vaping, it wasn't cigarettes. Leaves scuffed under my boot, and the wolf rotated his left ear towards me.

"Hey buddy, time to go back," I said softly. He twitched both ears, and resettled his back legs, as though he considered bolting and then didn't. "Sorry I left you today, had business. There's a deer haunch for you in the freezer, you'll like that, right?" He turned his head and met my gaze. To my eyes, he was visibly disappointed, and who could blame him? I crouched and put my hand out, and after several minutes spun away, he stood and came back to me with slow, deliberate steps, head low, ears canted. I clipped the cable to his collar, and clipped the other end to my belt. I checked on where the people were; still talking amongst themselves, some lifting their phones to the sky for selfies or signal. The wolf and I faded back into the woods, and none of them looked in our direction. I sighed and put my hand on the wolf's back for a moment. He looked at me, his head cocked, and then walked ahead.

It was full dark by the time we got back to the cabin. "I hope you're happy," I said to him as we walked towards the porch. He glanced at me over his shoulder.

Rachel was on the back porch, smoking a cigarette. "Anybody see you?" she asked.

"No, but it was close."

"You know, there's a reason normal people don't keep wolves as pets," Morgan said, banging out of the screen door.

"I'm shocked and disappointed that you'd call me a normal person," I said, stifling a yawn.

"You'll need that sheet metal we talked about, I guess," Rachel said, frowning at Morgan as she picked up the pack of cigarettes and shook one out. Morgan ignored the frown, held out her hand for the lighter; after a second too long, Rachel gave it to her.

"I will. There's only so long this can keep going, though." Really, I just didn't want him drugged up and stuck in a scientific facility for the rest of his days; I hadn't intended to be his jailer.

Rachel nodded, taking the final drag. She stubbed out her cigarette and dropped it into a metal bucket hanging on the porch rail. "Figure out what you want to do," she said, and went inside.

Morgan exhaled a cloud of smoke. "I kind of expected more."

"I did too." I listened, but there was just normal quiet conversation inside, nothing tense. Nobody complaining or angry, except maybe Everett for his lack of internet. "Maybe Rachel is learning that people other than her can make decisions, take responsibility." Actually, it would be nice if somebody else took this responsibility. I didn't know the first thing about wolf rehoming.

"Maybe." Morgan shrugged. "Trusting you like this is kind of a major thing."

"*You* don't seem too worried."

"Mostly because it's so damn funny." The wolf stood at the screen door and peered into the kitchen. He looked back at me, and then hit the door with his paw.

"I guess my prince is hungry. I may or may not have bribed him with frozen venison."

"That sounds reasonable." She sat down on the back step to finish her cigarette.

I brought the wolf inside. Sidney was tending to the pot while one of the hounds sat nearby, staring raptly. In the living room, Everett had one of the laptops open on the coffee table, and Sela sat next to him. Rachel was in a nearby rocking chair, one that had survived the wolf's tender mercies.

Everett glanced up, stayed looking at the wolf briefly. "Hey. I'm just showing some of the information that we got from the Silvernail stuff. It would be fascinating, really, if we'd volunteered for this."

"It's fascinating anyway, just in a different kind of way," Sela said, squint-frowning at the screen. "Sick fascination, I guess."

"So, the basics?" Rachel asked.

"First off, they're interested in what abilities we may or may not have. They've heard that we can change into wolves, somehow, but haven't ever seen it. They tried like hell to get Rachel to do it, but she didn't. The fact that we're stronger than we're supposed to be, have heightened senses. They pretty quickly got interested in the genetics of it. They've got Ward DNA, from stealing Bill's truck and vacuuming it for hairs. They've got Culver DNA now." Everett licked his lips, and glanced at me. The screen door banged as Morgan came in. "We already knew they did something involving Sela's blood, like they treated a male subject that they vetted before this, and then used his sperm to inseminate Dulcie's eggs. They got a viable fetus that they implanted in an unnamed surrogate. You knew that part, way back when. That surrogate—" he broke off a second, looking towards the kitchen where Sidney was, but with our hearing, everybody was going to hear everything, no matter what. "That surrogate miscarried, but they repeated the process. Except that the fetus is actually twins." Everett was blushing, but his voice was steady. "A boy and a girl."

We all looked at each other. That we knew of, Culvers didn't ever have boys.

"Does Bill know about that?" Rachel asked.

Everett looked down at the screen. "Um. No, I never told him anything about the babies part of it. Mostly that they had the DNA and that they were encoding that, and looking at individual abilities. Bill is concerned with how Silvernail found out about wolf families in the first place, and then specific individuals. What he's working on is warning other families he's in contact with, so they're on their guard and maybe moving around a little, for their protection."

"Why didn't you tell Bill?"

"I don't know. Baby stuff isn't really his business, is it?" Everett cleared his throat, and took a drink from the glass of lemonade in front of him.

"Thank you, Everett," I said, when it seemed like none of the rest of us really knew what to say.

"Bill doesn't need to know everything," he said with a sideways smile. "He just thinks that he does." Another reason for Everett to not mind so much, being sent with us. Besides, we don't know what kind of consequences he had to face for agreeing that on the last raid, the doors weren't opened for us the way they were supposed to be.

"Subversion in the ranks, you love to see it," Morgan said.

"Hey, uh, have you seen anything that said where the wolf came from?" I asked.

Everett rattled on the keyboard for a little while, hunching his head forward to peer at the screen. "It looks like they trapped him a year ago, on the New York/Canada border, more or less. Evidently they wanted to see if he would hybridize with the genetic material they had."

My stomach did a slow roll, and I didn't even need to look at Morgan to sense the tension that ran through her, like high voltage power lines. "We aren't animals."

"To Silvernail, all of us are animals. Or we were, until they couldn't crossbreed us with wolves. Now I guess we're just monsters."

"What about the surrogate? Where is she?" Morgan asked after a charged moment of silence.

Everett shrugged. "They don't say where she is in any of this, they're real careful about that."

Sidney came to the kitchen door, looking shaken but trying to hide it, drying her hands on a towel. "Food is ready, if we're hungry."

"It smells great," Joe said, getting to his feet. He'd stayed really quiet through the day; not that I knew him well, but it seemed like he was quieter than usual. Maybe just horrified like the rest of us, and eager for the conversation to be over. Maybe waiting to see if he was going to have to be on his guard the entire time around my family, the way he shouldn't have to be around his. And maybe the comments I'd heard weren't *that* bad, maybe they were just the kind of teasing that all of the Wards had to put up with when they were first being included in operations, but they seemed bad. I hadn't mentioned to Rachel, or anybody but Morgan, that Joe was trans. But also, I'd only had permission to tell Morgan, and that's what I stuck with. I was so good at borrowing trouble already, I didn't need to do it over Joe Ward too.

Chapter Seven

We spent a few days close to home, Everett trying to play it cool and act like he wasn't climbing the walls for lack of internet, Joe trying to fit in with our household unit. Sidney appeared to have taken up knitting, and was industriously creating a cradle blanket or something, I couldn't quite tell yet, while Sela and Rachel discussed what they were planting where. I wasn't pressed into service on that, probably because keeping track of the wolf was considered my full time job lately. That, and distracting Morgan.

Either she read my mind, or was hoping to interrupt a peaceful moment she assumed that I was having, because Morgan came out onto the porch just then. "What are you doing?" I asked before she could open her mouth. She looked startled to see me, but I didn't believe that.

"Hello to you too. What do you mean?"

"I mean what are you up to? Today." I knew the answer, but it was good to ask.

"Why?"

"I think we should take Everett to McDonald's for his internet fix."

"Not a bad idea, we can placate Sidney with apple pies."

"Why, what is she doing?"

"Oh, knitting and crying. She apologizes and says it's hormones, and not to pay attention to her. Then she cries some more."

"Think she misses her husband?" Or Dulcie. I kind of felt like I didn't have the right to cry about Dulcie. I wasn't around for long enough. We didn't talk about Dulcie, though.

Morgan shrugged. "Or it's hormones." She looked back through the screen door for a moment. "What has you so proactive, anyway?"

"I don't know. Nervous, I guess, now that I've seen the outside world again, and got reminded of everything. And I want to look up some other things. Well. I want Everett to look up some other things."

"Of course, other things." She laughed.

"Like where to send him, as a for-instance." I nodded at the wolf.

She raised her eyebrows. "Oh, you done already at failing with a wild animal?"

"What do you mean, already? It's been too long."

"Even better. Yeah, I'll find Everett." Morgan went back inside, leaving the screen door to bang behind her. That was maybe too easy; I should be bothered about that.

I brought John Doe around back and put him in the enclosure, went and got a frozen deer leg that I tossed to him. He picked it up, looked at me appraisingly, and stalked away to enjoy it someplace to his comfort.

Out front, the boys were loading into the Jeep and Morgan was laughing about something, Rachel supervising with the ghost of a frown. "I'll keep an eye," Rachel said, nodding back towards John Doe's enclosure. "Unlike Sidney, I can keep up with him."

"Thanks," I said. "I'll have Everett do his online thing and find a sanctuary that'll take him. They got those all over the country, there should be one close to us. Kind of close to us."

"They do."

Morgan *leaned* on the horn, and waved when Rachel glared at her. "We'll see you later," I said, and jogged to the car.

On the way, Everett cleared his throat in the back seat. "So, uh, I've been reading all this stuff, right? While we don't know where the surrogate is, we know what facility's treating her. Like, a subsidiary. If we can get in there somehow, we can thumb drive a virus just like the other place, and get their data."

"How are we getting into a place like that, where they treat pregnant ladies? Surely not the old fashioned way," I said, and I was looking at Morgan.

"Don't call me Shirley," she said, and for once *I* curled my lip at *her*. Joe laughed, but I didn't spare the boys a glance.

"So what's your plan, then? I assume you somehow have one, even though y'all only been in proximity what, fourteen hours?"

"Something like that." She looked straight ahead at the road and I smelled her lie, which I can't always do.

"We were never going to McDonald's, were we?" Maybe I was wrong.

"Nope. But your great idea kept me from having to lie to get you into the jeep." Morgan seemed so very pleased with herself, and Everett laughed in the back. I glanced at Joe; I couldn't tell if he'd been in on it or not.

"Morgan."

"Okay so we've got somebody in the Silvernail fertility facility that the surrogate is being treated at. This woman thinks that she's going to be doing an interview for a mommy blogger or a fertility journalist or whatever the hell."

"But instead?" I didn't have to ask, not really, but I might as well.

"Instead it'll be you and Hunter."

"Where are we getting Hunter from?" I had a dawning thought about how much trouble this could get us in, but actually I didn't really know how much trouble it could get us in. What was Rachel going to do, ground us? We'd been grounded already, for everybody's safety. What was Ardith going to do? 'Get in trouble' in the real world was different from at home, with Mama and her temper, and what I thought now was also her fear.

"Well, she'll meet us in northern Virginia at a motel or something for y'all to get into your interview clothes and make sure you've got the questions straight between you. The interview's tomorrow."

"Interview clothes?" I was in jeans and work boots. We all were. It was the smallest thing to question, that I could wrap my head around. This could be so bad.

"I told her what I thought your sizes were, she's bringing stuff for you."

"Rachel's going to kill us, you know that right?"

Morgan grinned. "Aw, she'll get over it."

"What do you possibly hope to accomplish? And how'd you organize this so fast? We don't have internet at the cabin."

"We don't but the ranger station a few miles into the preserve does. And they don't turn it off when they leave at night."

"Morgan." I never would've thought they could've snuck out of that house on Rachel's watch, much less with computers and cell phones, to get this all organized. Calling Hunter. In hardly any time at all.

"Well, we want this person to turn informant and let us know where the surrogate is, so that we can be there for the babies' birth."

"Are we kidnapping the surrogate, or just the babies?"

"Maybe both. Is it kidnapping when it's kids that were supposed to be with you to begin with?"

From the back, Everett cleared his throat and said, "I'd guess that Silvernail would be inclined to make proprietary noises about those children, particularly the boy. Not that I think they're *right*, of course."

Morgan only just barely curled her lip. "Of course. But let's not count our babies before they're hatched. The more we can learn about Silvernail, the more we have to take them down when it's time."

"Speaking of, Morgan, you always carry that much firepower in the back of your vehicle?" Joe asked, in a conversational tone. Firepower? I looked at Morgan, whose expression had not changed.

"Nothing wrong with having two, three shotguns when you're driving around. Maybe a rifle. I've got a couple of knives too, did you want to see them, officer?"

"No, we're fine. I just wanted to check."

"You got some kind of little netbook or something Allie can use while Hunter's pretending to interview this lady? Or your tablet."

"Yeah, that's fine. I've got a case with a Bluetooth keyboard, too."

"Perfect, see?" Morgan looked at me until I nodded, which I did sooner rather than later. She was still driving. "And you better not fucking answer your phone this time. In fact, just turn it off now, save us some ringing in our ears."

"Morgan, I—"

"No, you're the only one here who has a conscience and we can't let that fuck things up." In the back, Joe kind of sniffed, and Morgan raised her head to look at him in the mirror. "Problem?"

"No, we're good," he mumbled.

"Leave Joe alone," I said. "I don't know what conscience has to do with it anyway." I didn't know what she might think of Joe's conscience, other than everybody always knew more than me. Maybe Hunter was able to tell her all about all of the Wards we've met, and why would she bother to tell me? At least I was a little better at being a wolf this time around.

"You feel bad because we told Rachel one thing and we're doing another, except Rachel isn't going to *do* anything so we have to."

"How do you know Rachel isn't going to do anything?"

"Well she hasn't yet," she said, like it was that simple.

"She was recovering too, Morgan." She got shot too, I didn't say. She spent those days in a lab getting messed with, while we were driving around browbeating the Wards into helping us, I didn't say. "And this is a lot of information to take in. She needs time, and then her and Bill will probably—"

"Agree to do nothing," Morgan said.

"Bill doesn't gather all his intel for nothing," Everett said uncomfortably.

"No, but he sure likes sitting on it, doesn't he," Morgan said in a silky tone that was just crackling with threat. They had to, by now, miss that little book that she stole from Bill Ward's house, but nobody'd said anything. "Look, it's shitty to say but I'm gonna say it, someday, sooner or later, some of *us* are going to be the ones making these decisions, not them. And right now it's sooner." No further answer from the back. I turned off my phone.

The motel had the kind of sign out front that had square plastic letters that could be rearranged, and advertised stays at fifty dollars a night. Morgan pulled in next to an old diesel Mercedes convertible, top up, and the nearest room door opened even before she cut the engine. A compact redhead came out and gave us a wave. Ardith was taller, but there was no doubt this was Hunter.

She and Morgan hugged briefly, and their grins matched. I looked at Joe again; it would be great if I knew he and Everett would back me up if I didn't like what was going on, but of course, it didn't really matter. Not if I balked, not if me and the boys said no. Morgan was a force of nature, plain and simple.

Hunter turned and sized up the rest of us; Everett and Joe she knew what to expect. Me, her eyes lingered on for just a moment, before looking back to Morgan. "It's tacky as hell in there, everything's decorated with antlers, but the price was right."

"Everything?" Morgan asked.

"Every last thing. I can't wait for you to see it." She pulled out two keycards. "We're in adjoining rooms, I figured we weren't all close enough to just share."

"There's five of us," I said.

Hunter laughed and winked. "Uh-huh. I said all. Some of us are."

Joe cleared his throat, but Everett said "So anyway, we're gonna have to figure out dinner. And then we'll talk tomorrow's plan, right?"

"Right," Morgan said. "Hunter, you brought the clothes?"

"Yes, I brought the clothes. And we'll order pizza? They don't have room service, if you can imagine, so the other options are the gas station's convenience store, that McDonald's, or running into the woods and finding something on the hoof." Hunter didn't wait for a reaction, she flicked a keycard to Joe, and then went back into the room she'd come out of. Room service. I've never had room service. "We've got a door in the middle we can unlock, let's stop talking on the sidewalk like yokels."

When we left this morning, I thought this was a short errand run we were going on, but Everett had computer bags and Morgan had a duffle, in addition to the guns. I just had what I was wearing, and whatever Hunter brought for me to wear to our interview. I couldn't really claim that I'd missed the all Morgan, all the time experience that I'd had in the fall; compared to endlessly chasing the wolf through the forest, I wasn't even sure which I would voluntarily pick. "Quit it," Morgan said to me, as the boys went to their room next door and then they and Hunter fussed with getting the in-between door open.

"Quit what?"

"Getting all introspective. It won't make you any happier."

"Thanks for the advice."

"I'm serious. Spending time mooning over what is and isn't won't make you happier. What could have happened, what didn't. That kind of shit. It's much easier to keep it together if you think about the here and now. Think about where you are and where you're going."

"Well, thanks to you, I hardly ever know where I'm going."

"Nobody knows where they're going, in the larger sense of things. Just need to learn how to enjoy the ride." She turned the TV on and flicked through the channels without really stopping on anything. Everything really was antlers; the light fixtures, on the backs of the chairs, on the headboards of the beds. Antlers and birch logs with the bark still on.

They got the door figured out and Everett handed me a tablet in a black zip up case without comment. "Now what?" I asked.

"Mess around with it," Morgan said. I guess they got this all planned. "Visit websites. Bookmark things. It'll be better if it looks like you've used the thing before the day of the interview. Maybe you should start a new folder, and put a file of interview questions in it."

"I've used a computer before," I said. "Tablets too."

"I'm sure you have, but somebody who's a blogger uses a computer different from somebody who's done school papers. It's not too big a deal, because Hunter's the interviewer, but still."

"I'm flattered you needed me at all," I said, and Morgan rolled her eyes.

"We weren't sending anybody in there alone. Silvernail had me on camera. They didn't have you. We can't trust one of the boys to do this. Rachel wouldn't do it, neither would Sela, and you know that."

I sighed and tried to think, a hard thing with Morgan staring. "I know." Never mind how much we all looked like one another. Anybody who knew about us would know immediately.

"Good."

I clicked through a couple of places as Everett hovered, Wikipedia, Amazon, YouTube. "You think you'll be alright?" he asked.

"Browsing the internet? Yeah, I think so," I said.

"That's not really what I meant." Everett was a hard one to read. He didn't really socialize before, when we first met him, but he seemed good-hearted enough. He wanted to do right, I thought.

"What, infiltrating a Silvernail clinic in broad daylight and talking with one of the employees in depth? With a Coutard at my side? I'll be fine." Bravado wasn't my strong suit. "Besides, it isn't like you or Joe could do it. Just let me play with this."

"Alright, fine. Let me know if you need any help."

"I do need to find a wolf sanctuary," I said, which I thought maybe sounded like it came out of nowhere, but he nodded.

"Yeah, I'll see what I can do. There's places that take re-homes from people who thought it'd be a great idea to keep them as pets, we'll frame it like that. I don't think they'll ask too many questions we can't handle. I'll tell them that he's a rehome you got on Craigslist, so you don't know where he's from."

"Thank you," I said.

"What do we like on our pizza?" Joe asked. He'd gone through the drawers in the rooms and found old phone books but what seemed to be more recent menus. Recent enough to have Instagrams on them, anyway.

"Meat," Morgan said, and Hunter laughed and rolled her eyes. "What?"

"I mean yes but. We're just stereotypes sometimes, right?"

"You're the one who offered the on the hoof option."

"It's a good option," Hunter said slowly and smugly.

"So...just meat?" Joe asked, looking around. "Allie, what do you want?"

"Do they have anything special?" I asked. It was almost more embarrassing that I hadn't had a whole lot of pizza in my life than that I didn't really know how to werewolf right. Not a lot of pizza eating in my Southern fundie household. He passed me the menu without pause, though.

"Just don't get too weird, Allie," Morgan said, as if I couldn't be trusted with food decisions.

"How many are we getting?" Everett asked.

"Oh good question, we need enough pizzas for five ravenous beasts. Three? Four?"

"Three's probably good," Joe said.

"So meat, and whatever weird thing Allie wants, and?"

"Is pulled pork on pizza weird?" I didn't know if I'd ever heard of that before.

"Maybe, but it sounds great. If nobody minds more meat."

"Let's get a white pie with broccoli," Hunter said.

"Okay now that's weird, right?" I asked.

"Yes," Morgan said.

"It isn't!" Hunter laughed. "Allie, how could you?"

"I'm sorry!" We were all laughing; I didn't expect Hunter to be fun, actually. I thought she'd just be mean like Morgan mostly was. It was a nice distraction from how *worried* I was.

"Okay so I think that's settled?" Joe said, and Morgan bestowed some of her wadded-up bills upon him.

"It's settled. Now Hunter, show Allie the clothes you got her and figure out if they'll work or if we have to scramble for something else."

"I went thrifting and got preppy clothes and fold up flats, I'm sure they're fine." She handed me a bag. "Make sure it fits I guess."

"Thanks." I went into the bathroom and closed the door. I kind of felt like Morgan would've just changed right there, in front of Joe and Everett, but maybe I just thought that there wasn't a whole lot Morgan wouldn't do.

It was weird wearing pants that weren't jeans or pajamas, but the kind of grayish slacks Hunter brought me fit okay. The same with the striped button down shirt, and the little sweater that went over it. By fold up flats she meant the kind of shoes that I guess girls keep in their purses for when they switch out of their heels at the end of the night; they fit and didn't look too weird when I put them on with everything.

"You look okay," Morgan said when I opened the door, eyeing me critically. "We should put your hair up I guess? Braid it? Hunter, what do you think?"

"Yeah, we'll put it in a bun, that way they'll know as little about what it looks like as possible."

In the dresser mirror, I saw Joe looking at me and then looking back at the TV. "Is this about what you're wearing?"

"Yeah, kind of. I don't have a cardigan, and it's different colors. Morgan's good at sizing, though, isn't that funny."

"I think we're pretty close, is all," Morgan said. "Pizza's here." Headlights swept the room shades, and I had a tiny chilled moment where I thought what if it wasn't pizza, but then I could smell it.

"I'm going to get changed back. I don't suppose you had Hunter bring us pajamas too."

"No, but I raided your dresser." She could've done that at any time and I wouldn't have realized. She could've had that bag packed in the back of the Jeep for weeks. Ready for action, hoping for it. Praying, maybe, if she ever prayed. Morgan wasn't just bored, she was desperate to know why nobody was *doing* anything. And now we were.

Chapter Eight

Even as we ate, Everett was already engrossed in his computer. He typed rapidly, like machine gun fire, and he leaned closer to the screen every once in a while. I hoped that he wasn't telling the other Wards what we were doing and where we were, as that was sure to bring Rachel immediately down upon us. Or worse, just the Wards, without Rachel. My phone was off, and Morgan's phone was off, or silent, and I'd done a good job not thinking about it for a little while, but I could only imagine that Rachel was just sick with worry, and furious.

Without Everett hanging over my shoulder, I felt far less self-conscious in my web browsing. I spent some time googling Silvernail, and reading different articles about them. I found a web site on the fertility clinic that we were supposed to be infiltrating, and read about that. The testimonials of happy parents who had successfully used the Silvernail treatments were a little heartbreaking; they talked about their history before coming for the treatments, of stillbirths and miscarriages, and thinking there was no hope. I'd never really given babies much thought one way or the other. Sometimes I found it hard to coo about how cute newborns were the way most women seemed to. Some of them weren't cute, but were still a little weird looking from the ordeal of birth. To want a baby so badly, though, and not be able to have one is what Dulcie had gone through. I wondered if she'd known when Mama was pregnant, and when I was born, and then my brothers. I never had the chance to ask Dulcie about being a twin, or if any of the stories about twins were true, the connections they felt with one another. Maybe that connection hadn't been there, because Mama wasn't a wolf, but I found it hard to believe. Did Mama know when Dulcie died?

Thinking about twins made me uneasy, though. All of it made me uneasy, just one baby would've made me feel this combination of anxious and panicked that I didn't know what to do about. Dulcie's would be twins, sure. Before too long my vision started to tinge red at the edges, and my skin prickled. But it seemed to me that there had to be a hidden benefit, a reason that the Silvernail people would be happy to have produced twins from inseminating one of Dulcie's eggs. They couldn't have known it would happen, not unless they knew about Mama. I bit my lip and concentrated on my breathing.

"Allie?" Morgan asked. She'd gotten up and stood close to my right side. "What's up?"

"They have to have a reason to want twins, right?" I said. "Did they know Dulcie was a twin?"

"Dulcie was a twin? It doesn't say that anywhere in the files," Everett said after a momentary storm of typing. "I'd guess they didn't know, because every detail they had is cataloged." That consolation banished thoughts of Mama hauled off to some facility, my little brothers shot in their beds. They probably each had their own rooms by now, I thought, one of them installed in my deserted space.

Joe cleared his throat uncomfortably. "Scientists really like twin studies," he said. "Twins are a built in control group and experimental one. Like those brothers who were astronauts? And one spent a whole year in space? But with this, from the get go here, they'll see if both end up being wolves, or just the boy, or just the girl. And if only one does, they can identify the genetic wolf marker, and then figure out how to turn other people into wolves. Or turn their wolf gene on, if they've got it recessively."

"Who knew you would be into genetics?" I asked, my skin still prickling. But then, it makes sense that Joe would be particularly interested into genetics, a trans werewolf. Maybe I should be particularly interested in genetics, what with Mama not being a wolf and I am. Every family had rules but it seemed like the rules were mostly guesses. Or maybe we just didn't have enough babies, but the Wards had more than enough, enough that they got differences sooner.

"This is kind of fucked up to talk about," Morgan remarked, and I could feel her tension. In my experience, there wasn't a lot that bothered Morgan. Or she was better at hiding it than everybody else.

"It is, I'm sorry. It shouldn't even be happening," Everett said.

There was a long pause when I guess even Morgan didn't know what to say. I sat back from the screen and stretched. The more I concentrated, the more I'd hunched over and tensed up. I couldn't look at this anymore, or think about it anymore, for right this second.

"You all done?"

"Good enough, I think." I kept having flashes of finding Rachel in the Silvernail lab, of her telling us that Dulcie died. "I'm going to go for a walk," I said. Everett kind of grunted. Hunter seemed to be napping. Morgan looked at me a moment and then nodded. If we were someplace less citified, I'd want to go for a run as a wolf, but I thought that didn't seem like the best idea just now.

"I'll go too, if you don't mind," Joe said. He seemed very alert for somebody that I'd also assumed was dead gone asleep not a minute earlier.

"Sure, that's fine."

"Take your phone," Morgan said.

"It's in my pocket." Time to turn it back on, I guessed. I wondered how many missed calls from Rachel we each had. Well, after we were done with this interview business, we were sure to go back to the cabin and face the music. Better to ask forgiveness than permission, that was Morgan's motto. One of Morgan's mottos. Joe levered himself up out of the chair and shook his legs to straighten his jeans out.

"Bring back donuts or something," Morgan said. "This show is making me hungry."

"We had so much pizza," I said.

"Hours ago!" And Joe closed the door behind us as Hunter stirred and made a complaining noise.

"Just stir crazy?" Joe asked after we'd walked down the road a little ways. There was a sidewalk, and intermittent street-lamps.

"Some of it's the reading material freaking me out, and some of it's that I'm not used to sitting in a motel room. Or bumming around on the computer or watching television. Not even at home. Mama would chase everybody out, didn't care where we went, so long as we were getting sunshine and exercise."

"Dulcie, you mean?"

Crap, the Wards didn't know about Mama either. I forgot, with all the twins talk but nobody asking. "Yeah. Dulcie didn't abide people mooning around the house. If chores were done, then there was something else needed doing. Or the outdoors to enjoy."

"I imagine Sela didn't always need that kind of nudging."

"No, we were all pretty good about it, really. Sela..." I sighed. "What happened wasn't good for any of us. Sela took it harder than Rachel, to be sure. She used to stay closer to home, but she definitely never used to spend so much time just sitting in the house. Though Rachel seems pretty much the same. Maybe gruffer."

"Rachel and Morgan seem the type that keep their secrets close."

"Like mother, like daughter."

"So you're like Dulcie was? That makes more sense than when we thought you and Morgan were sisters."

"Morgan's sister is a doctor." I hadn't met Dr. Fran yet; Rachel took Morgan to her once over the winter and they returned without comment. It was days before they unthawed.

"She what? Wow."

We were quiet a little while, just boots scuffing on the pavement. "What about you, are you like your dad? Did we meet him?"

"No, you two didn't meet him. My dad is deployed in Afghanistan." Joe stopped and toed at a glint on the pavement, then bent to pick up a quarter. "Heads up."

"Make a wish," I said, and he nodded and stuffed it in his pocket. "That's got to be hard."

"It's what the Wards do. Family and military. God and country." We walked another little while. There were bright white lights ahead, probably the gas station that Hunter mentioned. "My father is big," Joe said. "Big guy, big voice, big presence. He's Bill's oldest son. I guess I'm not much like my dad, but we...We always used to get along all right. Before. There's a scheduled time every week when he can use the satellite phone, calls home. Grandma has a clock set to his time, and she stays by the phone on that day. When the phone rings, she turns on the recorder and gets the conversation down. Depending on who's around, she's the one who talks to him, but we write down questions we want to ask him, things we want him to know."

"That's Ward organization for you," I said. He looked at me to see if I was teasing, and I smiled.

"Yeah, I guess it is. There's comfort in it, I guess. Organization, that is. Truth is, I hate those phone calls. I listen to every damn one, but I hate them. I can't help but wonder if we're going to hear him die on one of them. They aren't still seeing a whole lot of action but..." he trailed off and shrugs.

"If he was sent to Iraq, I guess he'd be home by now."

"Oh, no, he was in Iraq first. He was home for two weeks and then shipped out for Afghanistan. War is where a lot of the Wards are most comfortable. Even if it's not really war anymore, officially. If it wasn't Afghanistan he'd go someplace else. He doesn't stay home anymore."

"That sounds like you all right," I said, rolling my eyes. He was quiet until we were at the edges of the parking lot. I should ask about his mom, but I can't make myself do it.

"I'm not going to do it," he said. "No military for me. Even without worrying about whether there's going to be a trans ban again or not."

"Not enlisting? Is that even allowed?"

He twisted his mouth and shook his head. "Yeah, I guess. I'll find something else. Local law enforcement."

"I'm not sure that suits you either."

"It doesn't," he said.

"Why not college? Seems like there's a lot of options once you can't take what everybody thinks is the easy choice."

"Grandma wants me to do college. Do a bunch of basic requirements at a community college, then pick a major and transfer somewhere else."

"It makes sense."

He shrugged. "Yeah maybe."

"Oh who knows, maybe we'll just have this weird shadow war that we're fighting for the rest of our lives, and then you won't have to worry about it." It wasn't that I didn't want to have a serious conversation; I just didn't know what to say anymore. And it was a worry, this weird shadow war. It was uncomfortable, to think that yes, we were the ones who had to take care of this. Who were we going to tell, that could help? That would take us seriously? That wouldn't turn around and do the same damn thing?

"I'm sure you think you're helping..." We both laughed.

I found Morgan's donuts and picked some up, and then went back and got more than I thought I needed. Maybe there would be some left for breakfast. I got my phone out when I got my money out and turned it on again, banking on the chances that Rachel wouldn't call in the seconds between when the prepaid turned back on and when I could turn the volume off. I had five voicemails; those were sure to be instructive listening.

We didn't talk on our walk back. Even with the company, even visiting the convenience store, I felt my head clearing. I wanted woods and birdsong and nature's silence. I wanted the wolf, even as worried as he made me. And I needed to find a safe place where I could let him go, because it wasn't with me.

Chapter Nine

As I got dressed for the fake interview, it occurred to me that it was my first time not wearing work boots since the night Kyle attacked me on the way home from the party. First time in something other than a tank top, or t-shirt, or flannel. I fiddled with the buttons on the shirt, not sure if I should do them all up or leave one of them open, or what.

"For fuck's sake, Allie, relax. Unless being an uptight poindexter is part of your character idea," Morgan said.

"Character idea?" I stopped fiddling and looked at her. I consciously made myself stop frowning.

"Your blogger persona. Your identity as Allison Glass. I don't imagine you're just going to waltz in there just like Alleluia Culver and interview her like that. You don't care about those questions. Or blogging. Or the Internet."

"Morgan, are you part of the werewolf CIA? You can tell me." I was still figuring out who Allie Culver was. Not that the Wards knew that.

"Well, I'd tell you but then I'd have to kill you." She laughed and ate another donut, some of the white powdered sugar clinging to the corner of her mouth. I pointed, and she licked it off.

I wondered if she'd listened to her voicemails from Rachel, if Rachel had bothered to leave her daughter voicemail. Now me, Rachel knew my sense of guilt, knew what buttons to press to get me to act. I listened to the voicemails all right, Rachel at first irritated and impatient, then livid, then even more angry, then worried. The worry bothered me far more than the anger did, and my stomach twisted as I deleted each one. We would go back to the cabin after this. We would pay whatever penance we had to as a result of this stunt, hopefully weakening the blow with whatever information we gained by interviewing Annie.

I didn't know how Morgan, or Hunter, or whoever picked Annie, out of the Silvernail employees whose emails she read, but maybe Morgan had a sense of weakness the way Rachel did, winnowed out the person who could have doubt planted in her mind and be the chink in the Silvernail armor for us to get through. Or maybe Morgan made it up as she went along, and she was just lucky. Or maybe this was a trap.

"Is she always so high strung?" Hunter asked. She'd just finished putting her hair in a twist, and was now contemplating mine. She had a pair of fake glasses that she'd put on, and when she said her outfit was like mine, she meant not at all, since she was wearing a skirt and a soft crepey blouse. She looked entirely different, with the glasses and the hair and everything. Werewolf librarian. I smiled, and she caught my look in the mirror and smiled back.

"Just when we're performing crucial missions outside her skillset." Morgan ate another donut. "So yeah, pretty much."

"Well good thing I'm the one doing the talking, right?"

"Right," I said.

"You have your questions ready?" Morgan asked her.

"I do, and don't start nagging me."

"I'm not nagging you. Just don't tell this Annie person anything. Please just remember that information is currency, and there isn't anything you're handing out."

"I know, Morgan. We all read the same declassified CIA interrogation manual from Vietnam."

"Oh I think we did, actually," Everett said. "Well, except somebody's real copy just got passed around." He handed over the USB drive with the virus on it, and I put it in my pocket. The same virus we planted in the Georgia computers, or similar enough.

"Yeah, ours was a PDF." Hunter pulled my hair back into a ponytail, turned my head one way, then the other, then did something that turned it into a low bun. "Pretty good, I think. Comfortable? Too tight?"

"It isn't too tight." I never wore my hair in a bun before. I never wore makeup either, but Hunter had swiped some mascara on my lashes and applied a little bit of eyeliner, and I looked very weird to myself in the mirror.

She turned to Morgan. "Okay, show me on the map where we're going. How long do you figure an interview ought to take?"

"The hell if I know. Until it's done?" Morgan held out the donut box, and Hunter took one and ate it delicately, hardly even getting powder on her fingertips, much less on her face.

"You're going to wait here?" Hunter asked.

"Yeah. Call this number if you need anything. Fresh prepaid, nobody else has it." Morgan passed Hunter a strip of paper. She looked at it for a few moments, then passed it to me. I got equal time with it, then she took it back and shredded it. Werewolf CIA indeed.

It hadn't occurred to me that Morgan wasn't coming with us, or Joe or Everett. Of course not. This was a fertility clinic we were visiting, though, a far cry from the barbed wire guarded Silvernail compounds we had previously taken by storm. I'm sure they would have security, but they probably wouldn't have guns. Maybe drones, but maybe not.

"You ready, kiddo?" Hunter asked. I sighed; she was Morgan's age.

"I am, Marion the Librarian. Let's get this show on the road." I'd kept up with Morgan, I'd have to keep up with Hunter.

Morgan gave me a short, hard hug and murmured in my ear. "What's my number, Allie?" I told her without thinking about it, and hoped that it would stay with me. "Go get 'em,"

"Be careful," Joe said, and Everett nodded.

"Yeah, you too. Don't play cards with Morgan, she cheats."

"I don't cheat, you're just not any good."

We got in the Mercedes and I buckled up. Hunter didn't drive any more slowly than Morgan did, and after all this time driving around in four wheel drive vehicles, it was strange to be in a car. I couldn't think of a single thing to say to her. The old diesel engine chugged strongly as we pulled up to the guard shack at the Silvernail fertility clinic. The guard leaned out and smiled. Hunter cranked her window down. "Morning ladies," he said. "What can I do for you?"

"We're here to interview Annie Timmons," Hunter said, answering his smile.

The guard picked up his clipboard and read for a moment. "Yup, I see you on the schedule here. Right on time." He reached over to hit the button to raise the little striped stick, and keyed in his radio. "Two ladies coming in for Annie," he said in a voice he assumed we wouldn't be able to hear. My window was open just a crack, and I flared my nostrils a bit as we pulled past the security shack and found a parking space. I smelled people, no dogs. New green leaves. Rain on the horizon, but not for another few hours.

"Hester and Allison," I said.

"I'll remember. Is this your first time playacting?" she asked.

"Yeah, it is." Other than anytime I'm with wolves who aren't Morgan and the aunts. She nodded and grabbed a little notebook and pen from her glovebox.

"Lock the door behind you."

The waiting room was airy and filled with light. The chairs actually looked comfortable, and the tables were full of glossy magazines, not ripped up older editions of things. The receptionists smiled at us expectantly, and I had an uncomfortable moment when I felt like they were sizing us both up, trying to figure out which one of us wanted to be pregnant. Then another woman came from a back hallway, just a little bit plump, with glasses like Hunter's fake ones, and a whole lot of curly hair. "I'm Annie," she said. "Which one of you is Hester?"

"Hi Annie, I'm Hester, and this is Allison. Thanks very much for seeing us, and so quickly." Hunter had a very good 'normal people' smile that she put on, I was surprised. She was much better at blending than Morgan.

"Oh, you know how PR departments are, they jump on opportunities and expect everybody to be excited about them." She motioned for us to follow her. "We lucked out and got the conference room to set up in," she said. "There are some lovely snacks for us there."

"Well, it just isn't right without snacks," Hunter said with a smile, and Annie laughed.

"I know, right?"

I flipped open the tablet case and pulled up my file to make a show of recording notes. My palms were damp, and I rubbed them on my pants, acting like I was straightening out the creases. I didn't see any cameras in this room, or in the hallway we'd walked down. There had only been a single one in the waiting room, up in the corner and following a slow steady arc. This place didn't smell the way the Georgia Silvernail compound had. There were no rabbits, and far fewer computers. The smell of disinfectant was strong, and those alcohol based hand sanitizers were mounted on the walls all over the place.

There was a plastic tray of goodies on the table, croissants and muffins, with a separate tray of individual butters and fruit spreads. There was a carafe of coffee, with accompanying sugar and creamers, and of course a water cooler with its cone shaped waxed paper cups, glugging in the corner. We were all a little awkward, and we laughed about that some, but I saw the glitter in Hunter's eyes, bit my lip, and then she got on with it.

We got through the preliminaries that I'd read on Wikipedia, when the company started, how it floundered around a little at the start without being affiliated with any other established scientific companies or labs. How Silvernail went off to Europe to fight in World War II. How the company made first aid kits for the Allied soldiers. The postwar boom was good for Silvernail, and it was in the sixties that they made their partial slide into fertility treatments, pioneers of the industry. Of course, they also had an interest in women's health issues, and birth control had been on their plate for a while as well. With longevity rounding this branch of Silvernail out, they really had their fingers in a whole lot of pies.

"But what does longevity have to do with fertility?" I interrupted, diverting from the script.

Annie blinked. "Well, you take it in small steps, I suppose. First step, if you're receiving fertility treatments and are artificially inseminated, you want the fertilized eggs to live long enough to get to the uterus, and implant. Then you want them to last the nine months until birth. Then you want them to grow up healthy and normal. But we've kept in contact with every family that has come through here, and compared their longevity data with samples and other data that we retained. After a while, the notion is that there will be a recognizable pattern with the people who have the more proven longevity."

"Wow," I said, then looked at Hunter and ducked my head to concentrate on typing my notes. Longevity was the Culver problem, that's for sure. I wondered if they knew.

Hunter picked up again, smiling. "This really all sounds very science fictional." Annie looked at her, trying to gauge the value judgment of the statement.

"We're trying to do good here," she said at long last. "We haven't figured out a cure for cancer, or at least this branch of Silvernail hasn't, though I'm told we're on the path to lowering an individual's chances of developing cancer during his or her lifetime. Somebody is also working on a delay tactic of sorts, though I guess that's an awkward way of phrasing it."

"A delay tactic?" I asked. Hunter cut her eyes to me again. If it was Morgan, she'd be grinding her heel on my toes under the table. I couldn't help but think of the special "vitamins" Mama had given me as I grew up, and my late initiation to wolfdom, at sixteen going on seventeen instead of Morgan's nine.

Annie thought for a moment, not noticing our silent conflict. "There are certain degenerative diagnoses that some people will receive fairly early in life. Macular degeneration, for instance. If we can push that back, or change it around, so that MD always becomes a late life diagnosis, that person's life is effectively very different."

"And what have your success rates been for that?" Hunter asked.

"Well, we've had trials with Rhesus monkeys, I believe. The monkeys and humans both get macular degeneration. We've worked with it both on a genetic level, at insemination, and with another experimental group have also tried fine tuning pharmaceutical means of mitigation from the get go. Like how some people with migraines take medication every day as a preventative, rather than only taking medication when they already have an active migraine."

I nodded and kept my eyes on the screen. I didn't like the suspicion I was having. Hunter asked a question I didn't quite hear for the rushing blood in my ears. To her credit, Annie maintained her upbeat tone, though I could tell she was casting glances at me, and I did my best to marshal my senses and just look as though I'd lost my place in my notes or something.

"What's the point at which you feel like these things will go to human trial?" Hunter asked.

"Oh, the FDA is very particular about everything, and extra strict about these sorts of things. I don't imagine we'll get any kind of green light for human trials until we're showing golden results on all of our trials. Thankfully, I'm not really in the experimental and research section, I'm more to do with people who come in for actual treatments. I don't need to go through all of that red tape!" she said with a laugh, and we laughed with her, lightening the mood.

I asked, "Do people come in with their babies, after they're born, so that you can meet them? I mean, if you've put in all of that work, it seems like you would sort of form a relationship with these families as they go through their treatments and pregnancies."

"Oh sometimes we get to see the babies. If nothing else, they'll send us a card with pictures. We try to make the pregnancies as event-free as possible, once they've taken hold, and not have too many more appointments than a regular pregnancy would have."

"But there are more?" I asked. Hunter couldn't tell me to shut up, Annie couldn't know this wasn't the interview she thought it was.

"A few more. Some blood draws, frequently we'll do an amnio, that kind of thing. Nearly everybody who comes through here knows the sex of their baby well ahead of birth, if not at conception."

"Do you end up with a lot of multiples? I've heard that happens with fertility treatments."

"The way it typically happens is because more than one egg is inseminated, and then a number are implanted, to have the greatest chance of pregnancy. Frequently the decision will be made to reduce the number of fetuses present after a certain stage of pregnancy, to give the most viable one the best shot, but not everybody does that."

"All this kind of makes me wish I'd majored in biology instead of journalism in college," I said, smiling and glancing at Hunter. She laughed and nodded on cue.

"College is full of choices," Annie said. "Not always the right ones."

"Oh, isn't that the truth." Hunter threw her head back and laughed, and we laughed with her. I tried to imagine what kind of a college life Annie had. Then I imagined Hunter and Morgan raising hell on a campus. It seemed to me that Ardith might've pushed her sister towards getting more of an education. What *did* Hunter do, other than get up to mischief with Morgan?

"So, what do you think of all this?" Hunter asked in a less formal tone.

"Well, what do you mean?" Annie asked.

"I don't know. When you go home at night, what do you think about the science magic of baby making? It kind of takes the romance out of things, don't you think? The slides and the petri dishes and the operations."

"When a couple struggles with infertility, it isn't about romance anymore. It's about a mother and father wanting a child." Annie shook her head. "No, we do a lot of good here. I don't really question our motives. It isn't as though we're playing God, we're using the tools that are already here for us to pick up."

"Do you have any children?"

"No, I guess I just haven't found Mr. Right yet," Annie said. There was something else in her face, or voice, that I couldn't quite read. She didn't smell anxious, not quite. Doubtful, maybe?

Hunter winked. "Who needs him, right?" We all laughed. "Would you use Silvernail's fertility services, were you in that sort of a position?"

Annie hesitated. "I'm not the right person to ask," she said. "Medically, yes, I trust the company's services. Personally, I don't know if I want a baby of my own. I'm an aunt already, and certainly don't mind that."

"Well, I guess that's everything," Hunter said. She'd had her little notebook open, but that was the only point at which she wrote anything down, before closing it. "I want to thank you again for being so awesome, and talking for so long on this topic. Once you get a few more babies under your belt, you should take pictures of the family and put them on the wall, like they do at restaurants." Hunter gave a smirky grin.

Oh great, I thought, but then Annie laughed. "Actually, that's something I can show you. As I mentioned, some parents have sent us pictures and with their consent, we do have a display wall for them."

"Yes, we'd love to see that on our way out," I said. I grabbed another croissant, because they were really good. I noticed that Hunter still had her paper coffee cup in hand, and had refilled it yet again. She saw me looking and flicked her eyes to my cup. I refilled mine, getting the last dregs from the pot. Our paper napkins were gone, but I don't know if Annie noticed; I assumed they were in Hunter's pocket. Annie finished her coffee and just left the cup on the tray. I flipped the tablet case closed. The flash drive felt like it was burning a hole in my pocket, but we hadn't yet seen a computer.

We took a different turn at one junction, and came along a side of the building that was all hallway with big open windows, looking out onto the lawn and an uncomfortably well-groomed garden. There were some chairs. "This is where some of our patients sit to prepare for treatments," Annie said. "It's beautiful, and it's relaxing."

"It is a nice area," Hunter said, sounding genuine.

The walls behind the chairs were starting to fill up with the pictures that Annie had mentioned. I wondered if it was the originals, or if Silvernail had made identical copies, to keep some on record. We walked through, trying not to seem like we were looking too carefully, though I didn't have a specific goal in mind. One of the pictures, I registered but passed over. Three steps later, though, I turned and went back. Hunter and Annie kept moving forward, and their conversation faded out of my ears as I stared at the picture; I'd passed over it because I knew it.

It was a picture of Mama, with her arms around Jason and Kevin, sitting on our front porch.

I remembered the day the picture was taken. We were going to the church barbecue, and Mama had just finished making some twenty pounds of potato salad, and was ready to go to the church basement and make fifty gallons of sweet tea. Daddy had the meat at the church already, ribs done marinating, hot dogs, hamburgers. We kids had shucked all the ears of corn required to feed the parish. Mama was wearing her favorite summer dress, linen with little blue birds on it, and she called it her June Cleaver dress, because it was kind of in a fifties style. She hadn't put her shoes on yet, though she never ventured barefoot into the outdoors, and her blue sandals were on the porch next to the rocking chair. The boys were in khaki shorts and button-down short-sleeved shirts, their hazel eyes like Daddy's laughing. After the picture was taken, they pulled out water guns and hosed Mama down. I expected her to pitch a fit about her dress, but she just went and put on a plain blue one instead.

I guess she'd sent it in because who knew her, and our family, that would end up coming to a fertility clinic in Virginia? It was funny, though, because I didn't remember anything unusual about her pregnancies. Doing lessons in waiting rooms, lots of waiting rooms, both pregnancies. More appointments than normal, she talked sometimes about the trouble, but I never had to stay with anybody while she and Daddy drove to Virginia, say. I was five when Kevin was born, old enough to remember. Had the clinic been in Alabama at the time? Did they come to Mama, was it Silvernail the whole time, every time we went to the doctor? Did the boys have female twins that they 'reduced,' to give the boys a better chance? The humming in my ears grew to match the humming of the fluorescent lights that were on above our heads, despite all of the natural daylight flooding in.

I smelled a wolf at my side, and turned my head just a little as Hunter touched my elbow. "Allison, you should know better than to drink so much coffee," She took my cup from me and stacked it with her empty one. "Funny you mentioned migraines earlier, she gets them from caffeine when she isn't careful," she said, turning to Annie, who was only on my periphery as not-wolf. "Let's get you to the car. Is there a room where she can sit while I pull around?"

"Oh, I'm so sorry," Annie said. "We could have done decaf if I'd have known."

"It isn't an all the time thing, just enough to be a pain in the ass." Hunter gave a little 'whoops I cursed' laugh. "Don't worry, we've got her medicine in the car, and she'll be just fine. Right

Allison?" I looked at her, and I could feel my pupils contract in the sunlight that reflected off of the shiny hall floor.

"She's right, it's my own fault, I'm sorry for the trouble." I put my head down a little. My fingertips were tingling.

"It's no trouble, it was really nice talking to you two. You can sit in my office for a second, it's right off the reception area." I could hear the smile in Annie's voice, and she led us through the halls.

In her office, Annie put me right in her chair behind the desk and stood off to the side a little, keeping an eye down the hall for Hunter to pull up in front of the glass doors. She seemed a little awkward, and I smiled at her in what I hoped was a distant enough manner to make the migraine story plausible. I'd never had a migraine, I didn't know what they felt like at all. Lucky that I had this miniature breakdown, though; we wouldn't have gotten access to the computer otherwise. "I've never had a migraine, but my sister gets them. They're just awful," Annie said after a while.

"They aren't a treat, that's true," I said and lowered my eyes again. Light sensitivity, that was one of the things I'd heard. The CPU for Annie's computer was under her desk, just near my right hand. She looked out of her office door again, and I worked the jump drive out of my pocket and thumbed it open. I leaned forward, just a little, and shoved the thing in the slot right before Annie turned around again. She looked at me, worried. At a guess, I thought she was concerned I was going to throw up in her keyboard.

"Here she is. Let me walk you to the door."

"I'm so sorry. I appreciate the kindness," I said, making an effort of getting out of the rolling computer chair so that I could pull the drive. Everett said it didn't need much time, I hoped it had enough. She never even glanced at her desk.

"I hope you feel better, Allison." Annie stood just outside the Silvernail fertility clinic doors.

"Like we said, no big deal," Hunter answered. We got over to the car, and Hunter put me in the passenger seat and made a show of digging a plastic pill bottle out of the glove box and handing it to me. I made a show of taking pills with the bottled water that was in the drink holder. She'd thrown the coffee cups on the floor in the back seat. Hunter got in the driver's seat, we buckled in, and pulled towards the exit.

I fully expected the guard from the booth to stand in our way, gun drawn. He remained in the booth and raised the striped arm, giving us a smile and a wave. Hunter grinned and waved back. Once we were on the road again, she put the pedal to the metal, and I could hear the old Mercedes engine's deep grumble as we ate up the miles.

"I'm sorry."

"It could have been worse," Hunter said. She'd taken off the fake glasses and thrown them on the dashboard. "You didn't do anything too bad or like, embarrassing, just looked like you zoned out, squinting and frowning. The migraine thing was good enough, especially since she mentioned the treatments just before that. Seizures were also on the table, but I didn't want it to seem actually like an ambulance emergency."

"I don't know how well I could fake a seizure."

Hunter waved a hand. "There are different types."

"Oh." I thought about that for a bit. I was feeling steadier already. It would be less of an emergency if I changed in the car, and that made the feeling fade even faster, somehow. I've only ever changed not-on-purpose the once, but because it was when I was the most scared I'd ever been, I couldn't help but be worried about it every time I got scared now. "I'm surprised you don't want me to explain myself."

"Honey, I already know."

"Do you really?"

"I do, Morgan told me. I mean, we didn't know this last bit about your Mama, that's a brand new surprise. We just figured if she wasn't a wolf, then she'd have normal boys the normal way."

"Nobody knew this about my mama." I thought about throwing up, and then I thought about how Hunter might react if I upchucked down the side of her vintage Mercedes. It was fifty-fifty, then I rolled down the window and the fresh air on my face helped me get myself under control.

"I guess we've got some answers, anyway. That's how Silvernail knew about you, genetically speaking. I'd guess she used her real name and all that, so that must've been enough to trace her back to New Jersey somehow. If she didn't just tell them, I suppose."

We were quiet for a little while. "So you don't think I'm some kind of a freak?"

"I think you're lucky your Mama didn't accidentally kill you with whatever it was she gave you to keep you from changing. I'm not saying that wolfsbane actually kills us, but it's named that for a reason." I stared at her. "No, I don't know what she gave you, or where she got the idea, whether it was from these people or not. But I guess it's questionable who she was talking to. Maybe she and your Daddy went to New Orleans on their honeymoon and talked to a voodoo queen or something?"

"They didn't."

"Well. That was my best guess, other than Silvernail. Though I guess it's hoodoo if it isn't harmful. Was it harmful? Hmm." And that's the last we said for the rest of the drive back to the motel.

We got out of the car and Morgan took one look at me before saying, "Oh Christ, what happened?"

Hunter laughed. "Nothing. We got the information, she did fine. We planted the seeds of doubt we were talking about, so I think it's just a matter of time before Annie there contacts us again."

"Really?" Morgan eyed me skeptically, also unwilling to say much more in front of Joe and Everett. "Because she doesn't seem fine." We smelled a certain way, after we changed into wolves. I hadn't changed, thank God, but I'd felt close.

"Too much coffee." Hunter was going to leave it up to me. Great. I'd save it until we got back to the cabin, to defuse Rachel. I hoped it would be good enough.

"Well alright then. Let's get you two changed, and then we'll check out and head back to our respective domiciles. Unless you want to come with me, keep Rachel from skinning us?"

"She might not shoot you before the skinning, if she knew that I was here," Hunter said. "In fact, maybe I should leave and then you should shower."

"Shit, you're probably right. We'll use the boy's shower, you weren't in their room at all." I didn't even think of that, Rachel smelling Hunter. I took the first shower, back in jeans and boots again, and meant to give Hunter the clothes back, but she was already gone by the time I was done.

"You want me to format this and put it online someplace for her to see?" Everett asked me, scanning what I'd typed on the tablet.

"God, if it's even readable, yeah." I couldn't remember a single thing that I might've typed, though I felt like I remembered the entire experience with uncomfortable clarity.

"What was it like?" Joe asked.

"Just like a doctor's office, I guess. Except nicer. Lots of money going into everything." I thought of the new magazines in the waiting room, I'd never seen that before. "Most doctors don't have gardens for the patients to sit in, I don't think."

"Yeah, I don't think so either."

Chapter Ten

We were about an hour from the cabin before Morgan turned her phone on again. I expected it to immediately scream into life with the wrath of Rachel, but it didn't. I figured that she'd have some kind of vengeful mother sense for when it could be used again. It was just the impression that she gave. Joe appeared to doze in the backseat, while Everett fiddled around with the interview stuff.

"Think we should stop at McDonald's after all, or will that be too much?" Morgan asked. She hadn't turned any music on. I thought about doing it, but just kept to myself instead. I thought about what the wolf may or may not have done in the past two days. I'd spent so much constant time with him, it felt weird to just run off without him all the sudden.

"I don't know about too much, with pies or whatever, but I'll want to use their wifi. We should've stopped and bought a hotspot while we were out, but then I'd have to figure out the VPN."

"Pies it is," Morgan said.

I imagined the scene at home. Sela and Sidney were certainly there. Rachel might have driven out to where she had service to call us again. Or she was sputtering angry, and chopping wood. Or she was furious and trying to track us down. Or—

"Allie, quit it," Morgan said, and shoved a milkshake at me.

"I just—"

"Yeah, I know. Just no sense getting worked up beforehand."

"I'm pretty sure she won't kill *us*," Everett said helpfully.

"She probably won't kill any of us," I said. "Which might be worse."

"You guys make it sound like my mother is a CIA torture expert or a warlord or something."

"Well, she is kind of a warlord," I said. Morgan glanced at me, opened her mouth, closed it. "Every family is its own mercenary group. Not everybody has an army like the Wards, though I guess every male family probably could. Or families that have both. Or whatever." I was not going to look at Joe and single him out.

"Do you even know how many families there are?" Everett asked from the back seat.

"Nobody does, except maybe the Coutards," Morgan said, turning onto the dirt road up to the cabin. "It's safer for everybody that way."

"If it's safer for everybody, then why the hell did we just send a Coutard into a biological processing facility?"

"We brought everything out with us," I said. "Napkins, our coffee cups. That's why Hunter had our hair back like that, so we wouldn't leave any. That's why the long sleeves, long pants. They could still track us from that spot with a dog, but I don't think we left anything they could find and get DNA off of. Out of. However it is you get DNA." What a good question though. Why did Morgan call Hunter now, and not when we were tracking down the aunts? Maybe because we had some answers now, we knew who the enemy was, and it wasn't the Wards. Or, not entirely.

"It does seem like magic, doesn't it?" Joe asked. He sat up and stretched, looked around.

"Science and magic are pretty close," Morgan said. She parked next to Rachel's Bronco, and the dogs came from the porch and the trees to sniff us. It hadn't been all that long, not really, but dogs knew time differently. Even as a wolf, I knew time differently.

"I'll be there in a second," I said to Morgan, and went around back. I assumed the wolf would be in his enclosure. I heard the front door slam as they went inside.

The wolf was lying on top of the shack in his enclosure. He turned his yellow eyes to me and his ears came up. I didn't expect a wiggle butt reunion, but even that level of recognition was sweet. He was safe, and hopefully I would hear soon from the sanctuary that Everett emailed, and get him someplace where he had more than a single acre of space. "I'll be back out for you in a little while," I said, putting my hand on the enclosure door for a moment. His head came up when my hand touched the wire, but he laid it on his paws again as I turned away. Unless Rachel did murder us all.

In the kitchen, a pot of something stewed on the stove, the fire down low, and a batch of cornbread was in the oven. The others were in the great room. Rachel hadn't started yelling yet, and I wasn't sure if that was concerning. Maybe she wanted to only do it once, with everybody present. It was hard to say.

I came in, and Everett had the tablet out on the coffee table. I guess he had the interview document open, to show them, and Sela and Rachel were both reading. Sidney was in one of the rocking chairs, the family Bible in her lap. "You've got to admit, Rachel, it isn't something we would have thought of," Sela said.

"I suppose that's true. You know, because of how Goddamn risky it was." Rachel didn't take her eyes from the screen, but I saw the tension running across her shoulders and in her jaw. Could smell the sour adrenaline in the air, and admire her controlled fury. All this time, all these years, to keep everybody safe, and look at what was happening anyway.

"Well, they're here now. Nobody was hurt."

Morgan smiled proudly. "Everything went just fine."

"You involved a Coutard, which could cause problems in the future." So much for taking showers so she wouldn't smell Hunter. "You went to a facility owned by a company or military force or whatever the fuck it is that has targeted us, for whatever reason. And you did it all just by disappearing for almost two days, without telling anybody what you were doing, and answering any communications. We had no idea what happened to you." Rachel's voice grew in volume as she went on, and I felt myself shrinking. "You had two Wards with you, which also would have put the rest of us in deep shit if you ran into trouble. And you had the potential to lead them back right to our doorstep. Again." I thought of the burning cabin in the pines, Dulcie's blood slicking the floor, and shuddered.

"Nobody followed us," Morgan said, utterly calm. "Hunter and Allie went in a separate car to the facility, from a motel. Nobody followed them back there, and then we got in our vehicles and went our separate ways. Hunter's license plate wasn't even her real one."

I thought Rachel was going to slap her, could imagine the too-quick movement across the room, the crack of her hand on Morgan's face. Mama would've slapped me for that, and my face felt hot at the memories, the anticipation. Rachel didn't move. "Which would thrill Ardith to pieces, should she learn that."

"I'm not sure Ardith didn't know." Ardith definitely didn't know, but Morgan loved plausible deniability.

"Regardless. Did you really gain anything? You have a bull-shit little fake interview to put on a website that nobody reads, you may or may not have made buddies with this Annie girl who might never say anything to you ever again."

"Two things," I said, taking my courage in my own two hands and interrupting Rachel's growing head of steam. She clamped her jaw shut and looked at me with blazing eyes. I steeled myself. She wasn't going to hit anybody. She was so mad because she was scared, not because we'd defied her. "First, I got a jump drive plugged into Annie's computer that will email everything on that computer to Everett. All of her emails, all of her data, and if her computer had any sort of administrative access, that means Everett will have that too, the next time he's on a computer connected to the internet." I paused and took a breath, steeling myself. "Second, I know how they found us in the first place."

"You do?" Sela asked, her voice catching. She couldn't abide all this anger either. Morgan was *staring* at me.

"There was a wall of pictures from happy families who had gone through successful fertility treatments," I said carefully. "There was a picture on that wall, of Mama and my brothers."

The quiet in the room was what the woods felt like after a gunshot, or a thunderclap. I waited, and then looked at Rachel. Her face was milk pale, her nostrils were flared, and her eyes had dilated. Sela looked similar, her hand over her mouth, and tears starting. Sidney had looked away, hands on her belly.

Morgan's expression was unreadable to me; I might as well not be talking about anything interesting. Maybe she was mad that I hadn't told her in the Jeep, but had carried my secret like a poison apple back to the cabin. The boys both looked grave, and a little confused; they thought Dulcie was my Mama, and they knew that the Culvers didn't have boys, and any number of other general knowledge, wolf family secrets that I'd only just scratched the surface of.

"Did you take it?" Morgan asked when nobody else talked.

"No, it was under glass, along with all of the others. But I recognized her. I remembered the day it was taken. The day I took it. I don't know if anybody else had any idea that she went to them for treatments. Even Daddy." I glanced at Joe and Everett; I didn't want to keep going. We were already teetering on some edge here.

"I know you boys are here to help us," Sela said. "But would you mind making yourselves scarce for just a little while? We have some things to discuss that won't really be comfortable for you."

"Yeah, that's not a problem is it Everett?" Joe got to his feet. Everett looked as though he would love to object, but licked his lips and stood up.

"Yeah, it's fine. We'll come back when you ring the dinner bell."

Rachel didn't ask where they were going, just followed them with her eyes as they went out the door. "I don't know how long we're going to be able to keep some of these details to ourselves," she said thoughtfully. "Your mama is out of the game, but sure ended up doing her family a bad turn all the same. You were a girl, and so she went to them so that she would have boys after. I wonder how she even heard of them."

"It's why they were able to make a boy from Dulcie," Sela said. She shook her head.

"But why is there a girl and a boy?" Sidney asked. "Even if a fertilized egg splits, it would make two boys, not a boy and a girl."

"Who knows? Why can we turn into wolves? Maybe it was so unnatural for there to be a boy, that when the split happened, it was a girl anyway," Morgan said.

"What it comes down to is that this information doesn't change much," Rachel said. "Your mama never knew about this place, so any knowledge of her, or from her, won't bring somebody here. We grew up in the pines, is how somebody could follow the breadcrumbs."

We were all silent for a moment. Sela's eyes held a shimmer of tears, reflecting the firelight. "It makes me wonder what we could have done differently," she said.

"It wasn't up to us. Our mama knew from the start that she was different, but she was our sister. Just not a wolf. The Nortons have twins exclusively, and they both come out wolf. I guess we just hoped that she would change when the time came, same as everybody else." Rachel sighed, and Sela shook her head, blinking the tears away.

"We loved her as best we could. I guess that's all there is to say." Sidney got up and went to Sela, leaning over awkwardly around her pregnant belly to hug her.

"You're kind of talking like she's dead," I said after another silent moment. Was there anything they were going to do, about Mama? What could be done? The damage had already happened, was already happening.

"She isn't a part of this family anymore, that's for certain," Rachel said. She turned and really looked at me. "But she already wasn't. We aren't going to go hurt her, if that's what you're worried about."

"I guess I kind of was. I'm sorry." I felt all shaky, but I also felt relieved.

"It's a valid worry, I suppose, but she's still our blood."

"I wonder," Sidney started, and then stopped. She laid her hands on her belly for a moment, brows knitting together. We all looked at her. "I wonder if your mama would have had the same girl twin thing, but she had the clinic get rid of them." She winced. "I'm so sorry. Oh I hate to even think about it. I hate everything about this."

"It's all right, I wondered that too. Maybe she did." Mama had always been anti-abortion, that I knew. But would it count as that, in her mind? Or would it be a way of removing monsters from the world before they could be born into it? "If Everett's computer dealie does what it's supposed to do, and if Annie's computer has either the information we're hoping for, or the access, or both, we'll find out."

"That's a lot of ifs."

"It's what we've got. It's not like I can call Mama and ask her myself." I still didn't know what she told Daddy in the first place, when she got back from dumping me off in Rachel's lap. I'd never know. "So, what do we do with this information about Mama? Anything?"

"We sit on it. There's nothing useful to be done about it. The hurt has happened, and hopefully the extent of the damage has been done. Even if your mama talked to Silvernail openly about the Culvers, there's only so much she knew about the Wards, or the Nortons, or the Coutards. Ivy's family in Ohio, sure, though nobody seems to have gone after them. And she didn't know other families, say in Florida, or Michigan."

"How many families are there?" I asked.

Rachel shrugged. "As many as there need to be, I guess. Just about everybody came to be in a different way, and we're scattered across this country. Lots of folks in the old country, too. Now, an interesting question is when the most recent family formed. I don't think there's been a single one since the Berlin Wall came down."

"Really? Why do you think that is?"

"There's only so many places people get hanged anymore, so that kind of takes the wolf strap option away. And people hardly make blood sacrifices to dark gods anymore, so there's that." Rachel cocked her head for a second, eyes distant, listening, and then relaxed. There were boots on the porch, and Morgan went to the door and came immediately back, followed closely by Everett, who actually looked excited about something. Joe trailed in last, thoughtful.

"We got another email from Annie already," Everett said.

"How do you know?" Rachel asked sharply.

"What does it say?" I asked at the same time. Rachel cut her eyes at me and glared for a second, hard. I looked away.

Everett opened his laptop and scanned the screen. "She wanted to make sure Allie was okay, for one." Morgan smirked at that. "She also said that she maybe had something else to talk about, off the record. She isn't really clear, and doesn't really seem sure. I think we picked right, but it might take a little while."

"Wanted to make sure Allie was okay?" Rachel asked, giving me the same look again. I sighed and squirmed.

"When I saw that picture of Mama, I was bothered by it. Hunter covered, said I got caffeine induced migraines. It's actually how I got into her office, and with access to plug the jump drive into her computer."

Rachel nodded thoughtfully. "All right then." Then she turned to Joe and fixed him with her gaze. "Where did you go for Internet access? I didn't hear any cars."

Joe blushed red right up to the tips of his ears. "The ranger cabin has wireless," he muttered after several moments of trying to keep quiet, or at least think of an alternative to confessing.

Rachel looked at the ceiling as though asking the lord for patience, a posture I was well familiar with, just not from her. Finally, she looked at Morgan, who was of course unabashed, and then she looked at the boys again. "Stay away from there," she said.

"Yes ma'am," Joe said mildly. Everett just kind of nodded, giving Morgan an unfriendly glance.

"Thank you. Now, you'll have to answer her, keep her on the string, so I guess pick a spot in the area where you can go have a cup of coffee or something and use the wifi. A diner near the highway. Tomorrow, take Sela with you, so that I know you won't ram off to Arkansas or something. With Hunter Coutard."

"Ma'am, what's our end goal here?" Everett asked.

Rachel paused; she probably didn't get ma'am-ed a whole lot, normally. "If I could burn every Silvernail property to ashes and then salt the earth, I would, but that just isn't feasible. Short term goal is keeping us all safe, and to be there when those babies are born, so that they're raised in their family. Long term goals, I guess we'll have to work on."

"Rachel I don't think keeping everybody safe and getting those babies are compatible goals," Morgan said. Rachel sniffed.

"That aside," Everett said. He kept his eyes carefully on his screen, as though Rachel or Morgan might turn him to stone with a glance. "Seriously. What we did in Pennsylvania and Georgia was damaging to Silvernail, but a company like that can rebuild easy. And while the data we got was useful to us, for you anyway, they almost certainly have offsite backups that aren't linked to the system in any way. Nothing we've done is going to stop them, short of buying them out and shutting them down, or driving them into bankruptcy somehow, I'm not sure what we're supposed to be doing." He paused, and nobody said anything. This sounded like he'd overheard Bill and Luke trying to hash out what to do, and was hoping Rachel had any idea. "If they hadn't found a way to get at the Culvers, it would have been us Wards already. Our attachment to the military isn't doing us any favors anymore. Or it would've been the Nortons, with how few of them there are. Or the Roarks in Nebraska."

"It isn't easy to fall back into obscurity, but wouldn't that be nice," Sela said.

"It's the information age. Everybody has cell phones, surveillance. DNA and blood gets collected and studied. People talk a lot about privacy, but there isn't actually a lot of it." I thought of running into Morgan's fans at Walmart, and them asking if she was really at that place in Pennsylvania. I tried hard not to look at her, because my face would give it away.

"Still and all, Silvernail isn't God, they can't be everywhere. We'll be careful, see how far we want to pursue any of this. They've already lost our trail, and they'll have to give up sooner or later. Ardith already let Ivy's people know." In the way of Rachel's declarations, nobody said anything for a few minutes.

Everett glanced at me. "Allie, the wolf place emailed you back."

"And?"

"They've got a six week waiting list."

"Great." Six more weeks of monitoring John Doe at all times, so he didn't endanger himself, or the rest of us. But it was an end date. It was better than nothing. "I mean, good. Thank you, for doing that. I got snarky about knowing how to use the internet but—"

"No, don't worry about it. It's nice to have a solvable problem sometimes." He kind of laughed, and that helped with the tension. What was done was done, what was said was said, now we had to live with it and wait.

Chapter Eleven

I wasn't out of bed yet the next morning when I heard Morgan and Rachel in the kitchen. "We need to call Fran, maybe get you in, see what all you should be doing for your hip."

"My hip is fine."

"Do you think I'm blind or stupid? No, don't answer that."

"Rachel, I know you're tickled pink that my big sister is a doctor, but she doesn't know everything."

"Neither do you. For instance, I don't have to worry about Frances going and—"

"Oh wait, I know, I can get started on some special exercises, and then do yoga with Sidney. Won't that be good for her, for when the baby comes?"

"Should I have made coffee first, princess? Would that have helped?" Cabinet doors slammed open and closed.

"I just don't know what you want from me. If it isn't one thing it's something else."

"I guess I just can't be happy if I'm not managing everything in your life."

"Well don't let me stand in the way of you and happiness."

I imagined everybody else in the cabin lying in bed, eyes open, listening to this. I imagined every generation of Culvers doing it, Rachel arguing with their mother Meredith, and on back up the line. John Doe raised his head and looked at me disapprovingly, flicking his ear towards the closed door when one of the coffee cups crashed either to the floor or into the wall. I got to my feet and to the door, and stopped with my hand on the doorknob. If Morgan and Rachel had progressed to whipping coffee mugs at one another, I wasn't sure I wanted to go down there.

"Have you two lost your goddamn minds?" Sela said from the stairs; I hadn't heard her go down the hall. I opened my door and slid out, shutting it behind me with John Doe still inside. Rachel looked up at us from the kitchen door, her eyes dilated so you could hardly see the blue. I couldn't see Morgan, but I smelled her in the kitchen.

"Just making the morning coffee, Sela, sorry to disturb you," Rachel said. I wondered why so many arguments seemed to happen in kitchens. It's where people keep knives. Sela glanced up at me, and I crossed the landing to the stairs and went down past her. Then I sidled past Rachel into the kitchen.

The percolator was beginning to hiss on the stove, and I was surprised to see Morgan crouched to pick up the pieces of the mug. There was an impact mark on the wall; I still didn't know who had thrown it. Morgan looked up, jaw set, and practically snarled. "What?" Her eyes were the same as Rachel's.

"Why don't we get out of here for a little while?" I asked. "Go for a run?" She stared at me a moment longer, shards of porcelain cradled in her left hand. I couldn't say I really wanted to know what she was thinking; I just had to get her and Rachel apart. I had to do something about all the tension from the past few days.

"Yeah. Let's do that." She stood and dumped her handful of mug into the dustbin, then stiffly walked out the back door. I glanced at Rachel, who by then had Sela at her side, talking quietly in her ear.

"We'll be back," I said. Rachel took a deep breath, sighed, and nodded. I listened a second, but didn't hear the boys. I didn't kid myself they hadn't heard, but if their choice was to lay low, I was glad. Sela caught my eye and gave me a tight smile.

Out back, Morgan had already changed, her clothes a tangled pile on the hard packed dirt next to the porch stairs. I was barefoot, in pajama pants and a tank top, and hesitated a minute even though this was my idea. She looked at me and chuffed through her nose impatiently, mouth hard, and then turned toward the woods. I shucked out of my clothes and closed my eyes briefly, thinking four legs, thinking wolf. To be fair, I hadn't yet failed to change when I wanted to, but my second nature wasn't exactly second nature just yet. I wondered if it ever would be.

As soon as I was done, Morgan came and shouldered against me, and then took off for the tree line. I followed, watching her gait. Physical therapy hadn't occurred to me, but I'd never had to recover from a bullet wound before. Morgan just liked to think she was invincible. I was content to let her set the pace and the route, and didn't have nearly as much trouble keeping up with her as I used to. She brought me past the still, which I hadn't visited recently, and right up to the property line where it butted up to the nature preserve. I stopped and laid my ears sideways; she looked at me with her head tilted, panting. I held her gaze a moment, and then turned off away and started running again. No guarantee that she was going to follow me, but I didn't want today's 'fuck you' to Rachel to include much more than it already had.

I heard her behind me after a little while, and when she passed me, I chased after her, shouldered past, and was out front until she laid on some more speed and jumped fully on my back. Somehow, Morgan always had more speed. We piled up in a hollow full of blackberry brambles, pawing and smacking our muzzles against each other, the brambles pulling tufts out of our fur. I squealed a little when she got my ear in her teeth, but I didn't think she'd drawn blood. I twisted and got hold of a mouthful of ruff that I shook back and forth, and then we both let go and stood a few feet apart, sides heaving and tongues lolling.

We were close enough to the cabin I could hear Rachel and Sela still talking, in the kitchen I thought at first, but then I smelled Rachel's cigarettes and knew they were on the back porch. Sidney was outside somewhere too, talking to some of the dogs who were circulating. I remembered John Doe was still in my room and sighed. Morgan lifted her nose just a little and sniffed. Her eyes narrowed, and she trotted towards the front of the cabin. I wondered what I'd missed. I watched her gait again, and could see the slight hitch, but she was moving much more smoothly than when we started.

Everett and Joe had just come out the front screen door, swinging it quietly closed, when we left the wood line. Morgan curled her lip, and it wasn't in play this time. They each had a laptop bag slung over their shoulders, and Everett was fiddling with his smartphone. Joe saw us first and put his hand out to stop his cousin. "Morning," he said, clearing his throat. Morgan lifted her chin at them, and I could see her hackles starting to come up.

I think Everett was willing to wait us out, keep his mouth shut until we'd gone off to change back, something like that. Joe, though, didn't stand more than a few minutes of silence.

"We just wanted to sit out here, be ready to go when you came back," he said. "Plus staying out of Rachel's path seemed like a good plan."

I tilted my head, because for one Rachel could undoubtedly hear the conversation on the front porch, and for two I hadn't thought that the boys were going to be involved in our trip to a diner with Sela. Maybe I had misunderstood. The phone in Everett's hand buzzed, and he looked down at it. Morgan gave kind of a growling yip, and I heard the back door slam and boots stride through the cabin. "There's only so much of this I can take before I start ventilating people," Rachel said as she came outside. She pointed at me and Morgan. "Go and get clothes on." She held the door open for us to go past inside. "Sit your asses down," I heard her growl at the boys as I got up the stairs. I'd never climbed stairs as a wolf before, it was weird. Four legs, not two.

I nosed my room door open. John Doe was on his feet, head slung low, hair brisling. His lips peeled away from his gums and I heard the rumble start in his chest. I turned my head away from him, looking down, and closed my eyes. I'd never had to time how fast I could change, but thankfully, it ended up being fast enough. I crawled into the room on my hands and knees, kicked the door closed, and stood up. The wolf looked utterly baffled and it would've been funny if I hadn't been so scared for a second.

"Sorry buddy, it couldn't be helped," I said. I found an elastic to wrangle my hair, and then I rummaged around for clothes and pulled everything on hurriedly. The wolf hopped on my bed and lay down with an audible sigh, still staring at me. I guessed it really was a good thing I hadn't changed around him before.

I heard Morgan on the stairs right as I laced my boots up, and I opened my room door. "Going to put him in the pen, I'll be right there," I called. She grunted in reply. The wolf kept his distance from me, going stiff when I put the collar on him to bring him out. Even when I put frozen chickens in the enclosure with him, he kept fixing me with a strange gaze.

Out front, the boys were still seated on the porch. Rachel had Everett's smartphone, occasionally poking at the screen with a finger. Morgan read over her shoulder, and glanced at the boys once in a while. "What's up?" I asked.

"You two are still going to check your email or whatever the hell with Sela. These two are staying here. Maybe I'll have them dig a ditch or something. Sheet metal the wolf enclosure."

I opened my mouth, closed it, looked at Morgan. I didn't doubt that she'd explain in the car. Joe looked appropriately shamefaced, though Everett seemed miffed at having been caught. I wondered why we'd spent so much time driving around trying to get Internet if Everett's phone just worked here; none of our burners did. Sela came out on the porch slowly. "Morgan, we're taking your Jeep?"

"Yeah." Morgan took one last look at the phone's screen. "You sure we should still go?"

"Go on. You've set this plan in motion, might as well see if it works. Truth be told, I didn't have any other ideas that were going to pan out." Rachel held a button down on the phone until the screen went black and put it in her back jeans pocket. "Come on boys, let's get cracking."

"We don't have to listen to you," Everett said. He sounded like one of my little brothers; even I almost laughed. Joe was already on his feet. Rachel stopped and looked at him, an eyebrow raised.

"Don't you?" To his credit, Everett held her gaze for a few moments. Then he licked his lips and looked away. "Bill Ward put you in my care. That says you have to listen to me."

"Yes ma'am," he said after a long moment. Morgan laughed and rattled her keys out of her pocket, and he shot her an angry look that just made her grin more broadly.

"Y'all ready?" she asked me and Sela.

We almost drove past the diner that Rachel mentioned, but then Morgan turned into the parking lot at the last moment, tires squealing gently. "Morgan, really?" Sela asked, but by then I'd seen the little tin sign in the window Wifi Access Here.

"Sorry Sela," Morgan said, and this time, she *did* sound sorry. The aunt I'd spent the least time with, she'd also seemed so distant once we'd gotten to the cabin, subdued. Rachel had that tempered spark of wildness, with some anger, that kept her going.

We got set up at one of the tables, coffee ordered, and Morgan read the emails. "It's amazing how fast spammers find an address," she remarked. "We're getting them already. Must be because of posting that article online."

"Must be," I said. When the waitress came back, I got the biggest breakfast meal that they had; my stomach felt like it was barking at my spine. Morgan got the same, Sela slightly less. I guess she didn't like sausage as much as the rest of us.

"Do you think this Annie can be trusted?" Sela asked.

"She can if she's really unhappy with Silvernail. There's no way to know if she's double crossing us, but you said she seemed genuine enough, right Allie?"

"I thought so, yeah. She smelled it. She seemed to really want to help people with fertility problems, anyway. I guess that's what makes her a good point of contact, if she's uncomfortable with the experimental end of things. I'd guess she hasn't had to deal with parentless test tube babies before, and Silvernail doesn't strike me as a warm and fuzzy guardian."

"It's still hard to accept that your mama would do that kind of a thing." Sela looked into her coffee, not at me.

"She was afraid, I guess. I'm having a hard time too. Have been since...everything."

"Are we all going to talk about our feelings?" Morgan asked. "Should we go to Applebee's and get cocktails? Are Cosmopolitans the right one for the occasion?"

"Can you behave for once?" Sela asked, not sharply, just as a genuine curiosity.

"Can't see how I'm misbehaving. Crying about Allie's mama isn't going to change that she's the reason these guys caught wind of us, and it's not going to change that she dumped Allie in the pines with nary a glance over her shoulder."

"She didn't seem *happy* about it, anyway." I couldn't stop the reflex to defend Mama. I wasn't even mad at her anymore, or at least not right now; just sick and sad when I thought about her. I tried not to think about her.

Morgan shrugged. "Anyway. Because we asked Annie about the experimental end of things, in 'hypotheticals', she's talking about the kinds of projects that Silvernail might be working on. She'll deny all knowledge, of course, should we publish that kind of thing. Good thing for miss potential whistleblower that we aren't even actually journalists, much less ethical ones."

The food came, and the waitress left us a coffee pot. Morgan kept reading the screen, wiping her fingers frequently to keep grease off of the laptop. "They make good coffee," Sela remarked after a while.

"Anything you want to do while we're out, Sela?" I asked. Morgan glanced at me a moment then went back to rattling on the keyboard. I pulled Morgan's untouched coffee over and shook in the requisite four sugar packets.

"Me? Oh, I don't know. Maybe the grocery store?"

"We could do that too. I just thought you might have someplace you wanted to go for fun. Much as we want things to move along, we've got a lot of time to kill."

Sela smiled. "Well, this is fun. I don't have anywhere I want to go, no. Fun is for you kids, I had my time."

It was about the last thing I expected to hear out of anybody's mouths, much less one of my wolf relatives. I took a breath, and out of the corner of my eye, saw Morgan shake her head, just barely. I finished stirring Morgan's coffee and slid it back in front of her. "What news, cuz?" I asked. Across the table, Sela relaxed, just a little.

"Pretty much nothing. Annie's still playing things pretty close. I'm asking her if she'll talk to the surrogate, see if she'll give us some kind of anonymous exclusive or whatever bullshit, and then we can get out of here." She picked up her coffee, drank half of it in one go.

"What made you decide to go with web writer instead of lesbians seeking children?" Sela asked. Morgan made a noise that I could only describe as a guffaw; some of the other diner patrons turned around and looked at us for a moment.

"Truth be told, I never thought of that. See, next time we do spy operations, we invite Sela along. She's smarter than us."

Sela laughed. "Morgan, you're too hard on yourself." The waitress dropped our check on the table and cleared some of the plates. Morgan closed the tablet case, the last slice of bacon sticking out of the corner of her mouth like a cigarette.

"I am my own harshest critic," Morgan said. She dug around in her jeans for cash; I never saw anybody else who wadded up their money on purpose, but maybe that was how Morgan kept new bills from sticking together.

"I'm going to use the ladies' before we leave," Sela said.

"We'll wait out front." Morgan led the way, grabbing a toothpick from the dispenser at the counter. They also had a bowl of lollipops, like you'd get at the bank, and I picked a red one. "So, it's not like Sela's a shut-in or anything, but she never wants to go anywhere. Never has." I unwrapped my lollipop and stuck it in my mouth. "Well, not never. But not since getting back from the world."

"Meaning after her love affair ended and she had a kid?" I threw the wrapper in the ashtray by the door.

Morgan put her sunglasses on. "He died."

"Oh." I was glad I hadn't pushed the issue with Sela. Truth be told, before the cabin, I hadn't noticed that she was home all the time. Or only left with the other aunts. I thought she was staying close to Sidney, and shaken up from her Silvernail experience. "How?"

"Car accident," Morgan said. She'd taken a Pennysaver from the rack and was shuffling through it. "So, I wonder if this

Annie thing is going to pan out. I wonder if we should give her some info on the bad side of Silvernail."

"I don't see how we can do that without telling her who we are."

"There are some articles I've found. Ethics committees. People wondering what that compound in Pennsylvania was that I supposedly went Patty Hearst at. Thanks for keeping that under your hat by the way, I wasn't sure you could do it."

"Me neither." I sucked on the lollipop for a second. "So, by saying you wonder if we should give her some info, you mean you already did, right?"

Morgan grinned. "You're catching on." Sela came outside, unwrapping a yellow lollipop. "Ready to go to the store?"

"I am. It's a pity we don't have chickens here."

"Sure is," Morgan agreed. I climbed in the backseat and let Sela have shotgun. Morgan left the radio off as she drove, and Sela gazed out the window without talking. I knew better than to think Morgan couldn't surprise me, but I never thought she'd surprise me by being sensitive about something like feelings. That just seemed out of reach for Miss More Human than Human. "Want one of us to come in with you?" Morgan asked when we pulled into the parking lot of the store. There used to be a sign, I was sure, and there was still neon in the window that spelled OPEN.

"I'll only be a minute," Sela said. Morgan and I watched her cross the cracked, bleached out parking lot.

"Should I ask what step we're actually to, communications wise, or are we saving that for family meeting time?"

"Annie is starting to get less than a sterling view of her beloved Silvernail, that's for sure." Morgan flipped her phone open, looked at the screen, then closed it and tossed it on the dashboard, lit a cigarette. There were times she needed to be constantly in motion and fiddling with things, other times not. I couldn't track what those times were, yet. I wasn't confident I ever would be. "Maybe she was already getting jaded."

"Who does she think we are?"

"She still thinks that we're just journalists that caught whiff of an evil corporation."

"Probably best to keep it that way, right?"

"I'm sorry, *you're* worried about *me* blowing our family's carefully guarded secret?"

"Morgan, there's honestly no telling what you'll do or say from one moment to the next. Not from where I'm sitting, anyway. Maybe you've got some plan in that crazy head of yours."

"A method to my madness?" She grinned at me in the rearview mirror. Her sunglasses were too dark to see her eyes at all.

"It's some comfort to me to assume that, yeah." We didn't talk for a little while. The parking lot was pretty empty, but for some kids sitting on the curb near the payphone, smoking cigarettes. "I also somehow trust you pretty much completely. I'm not sure how that works."

"Me neither, cuz, but thanks." We both laughed.

Sela came back with a pair of paper grocery bags in her arms. "It's hard to think of meals for quite so many of us," she said.

"Not more chili, I hope," Morgan said.

"No, macaroni and cheese and fried chicken."

"I think Rachel's working on the chickens thing."

"It's likely to be on her list."

"Speaking of her list, you figure the boys will be staked out for the vultures?" I asked.

"Nah, she won't hurt them," Sela said. "No matter what they do. It's a point of honor."

"Just make sure they don't realize that," Morgan said over her shoulder.

"Me? Never." I trusted Morgan, apparently, but she sure didn't trust me.

Chapter Twelve

There was more back and forth, two more days of email enticement which seemed to get really serious on her end really quick, and then Annie wanted to meet someplace other than the fertility clinic. "Looks like you need another poindexter outfit," Morgan said with a grin.

"Great," I said. "I'm just worried I'm gonna say something that tips her off. Or that she's going to look at that picture of Mama in the hallway before she sees me again, and she'll know that way."

"Don't borrow trouble," she said, surprisingly mild. "Just Hunter'd go do it, but they're supposed to be neutral."

"It doesn't affect just us anymore. It's us, and the Wards, and whoever's next. Nobody can stay neutral knowing that."

"People, even wolves like us, are real good at compartmentalizing," Morgan said. "Now let's see what clothes we can rustle up for you before we head out."

"Are we going to tell Rachel?" I asked. "We're just going to go?"

"I'll leave a note on the fridge," Morgan said, and I laughed.

"Oh, good, she'll really kill us this time. Leave our bones to bleach in the nature preserve."

"Here, read the emails while I drive." I went over what "Allison Glass" and Annie and Hunter discussed, and really, it hadn't seemed to take very much at all to get Annie to relax completely, and be pretty straightforward about how sometimes her employment felt a little off. And she was on the team for the surrogate, something we couldn't have even hoped for, really.

"Morgan, does this seem a little too good to be true?" I asked.

"What, like they're reading the emails and totally setting us up?"

"Yeah, maybe." She shrugged. "But what else are we gonna do? Even if it's a setup, if we're smart enough or fast enough, whatever, we can still gain from it."

"And if we're not, we're going to be in white rooms with our heads shaved and cameras on us while they try to get us to change."

She swung into a strip mall parking lot and turned off the engine, looked at me. "You still having trouble with that? Coming all over with that feeling?"

"A little. Last time I did was when I saw Mama's picture in the clinic."

"Gotcha. So always terrible times."

"Yeah, pretty much. I guess it makes sense, given..."

"I didn't forget about that, by the by. Just try and sit tight."

"Alright," I said.

"Now go on in and find something preppy to wear like Hunter did, I'll be a good girl and try to call Rachel." I went into the store, a consignment shop that smelled like incense and Febreeze. I don't think I took too long, maybe twenty minutes, half an hour. I'd basically found another pants-shirt-sweater combination that was a lot like what Hunter brought me. I was worried about shoes, but it turned out she'd brought the flats.

"Now, is Hunter going to be available?" I asked, as I changed clothes in the back seat.

"Already texted her. We'll park about a block away, and you can hop in her car and go to the diner where Annie wants to meet."

"It's a little scary how good you are at organizing this sort of thing."

"I know, right? Makes me wonder if I should get into politics."

"Oh God."

"Right?" She grinned at me, white teethed and happy, "Oh, or maybe the FBI? They got an age cutoff though, don't they?"

"I don't really want to talk about that right now. Or ever, maybe."

"Aw. Missed opportunities." Then she popped another tape in, and we didn't have to talk about anything, even though I wanted to ask her if she ever got tired of listening to her own music. Or maybe it was just part of some elaborate Morgan-game, the threat display of her everyday existence, where of course she had to be the best and the brightest of everybody in the room and fuck you if you didn't think so. No wonder she went away, went on tour, only came back to her mother and aunts sometimes. They'd've come to bloodshed before now, if she hadn't. Anyway that wasn't fair, it wasn't always Howling on the tapes. That was just what became the most familiar fastest.

I tried to think about what I was going to say, how far I still had to pretend I was some kind of freelance web writer. We didn't have any of the stuff with us even, a laptop, a tablet. Just me. Maybe Hunter would bring her little notebook. Maybe this was how investigative reporting actually felt. You just did things in the moment and hoped the important things would stick in your memory. But no, that couldn't be how it worked at all, because then it'd just be hearsay. Phones, Allie, people used their smartphones.

I fretted like that for most of the drive, Morgan singing along with the songs, though she *did* change the tape eventually and it wasn't Howling anymore. I didn't comment, and did she seem a little disappointed? I think she did, but I didn't know what she wanted. And then we parked on what looked to me like a random residential side street. "Are we—?" I started to ask, and then Hunter pulled up alongside us, leaned over and rolled her window down.

"Perfect timing," she said. Her hair was twisted up same as before, and she wore those fake glasses again.

"Always," Morgan said to her. They both laughed, and I slid out of the Jeep.

"Well, I guess I'll see you...when we're done?" I said when I came around the car.

"Be careful. I'll be right here." I didn't want to say Morgan was comforting me, but there was no way she couldn't smell my anxiety, and so that's really the only explanation I had.

"Careful as I can be," I said.

"We'll have things in hand," Hunter said. They exchanged another look, then Hunter pulled away.

Hunter had music playing too, and I wasn't surprised that her old convertible had a tape deck. What surprised me was she was listening to classical music, and I laughed and shook my head. She looked at me over the tops of the fake glasses frames, eyebrows raised.

"Sorry, it's just...you know Morgan the metalhead," I said.

Hunter laughed, and she had that same wildness to her that I was sure I'd never attain. It was like city mouse and country mouse, except they were the werewolves for life and I was the late bloomer. "I do know," she said. "And it can make it hard to think. And there's one song that always gets stuck in my damn head."

"Which one?" I asked, grinning.

"The bonfire one, I don't remember what it's called."

"Oh, I know it, though." We both laughed. "Does Ardith know you're here?"

"Big sis once again does not know I'm here, no. So let's try not to do anything stupid that'll get me in trouble, yeah?" She actually winked at me.

"I don't know what we could possibly do that would," I said. Never mind this whole thing in the first place.

"Still."

The diner was one of those chrome things that looked like a train car that fell off the end of the line. Hunter parked on the end near the road, simple enough to just drive away again without any maneuvering necessary. The windows had slatted blinds and little lace curtains, and as we walked inside, we could see Annie, but somebody else sitting with her, another woman. Hunter stiffened, maybe only enough that I could see it, but waved the waitress away and walked over to the booth, and I followed her and we both slid in. "Nice to see you again," Hunter said, her smile fixed.

"You too," Annie said distractedly. She glanced from me and Hunter to the other woman, who smelled like Sidney but not, and then I realized she was pregnant. They had food in front of them, barely touched, sandwiches and fries and stuff.

Acrid coffee in front of Annie. "This is Beth," she said. "I hope you don't mind I brought her but I wasn't sure what else to do."

"It's fine, just keep calm, and tell us what's going on," Hunter said evenly. She had her phone out in her lap, fingers barely moving. Texting Morgan, I hoped. There were lots of ways for this to go bad, and maybe only a couple for it to go good. Maybe it was already bad, or already exactly what we hoped for.

"I guess...I guess I've been kind of stupid," Annie said. "There were things going on that I didn't really realize. And Beth is unfortunately part of those things. She's acting as a surrogate mother for the company, carrying twins, and I knew all of that of course, but I didn't realize just how unusual the situation was. I'm not sure of the whole story, I'm sorry, but it seems like the real mom died and that's why they needed Beth." I couldn't stop my sharp intake of breath, but I guess it was the right thing to do, to act believable, like I didn't know that's how this had gone.

"The real mother died?" Hunter asked in a shocked tone, but none of the rest of her was. It was enough to fool Annie. Beth was looking back and forth between all of us. "So where will the babies go?"

"I don't know," Beth said. "That's my problem. The money's good, but...not *that* good. And when I asked Annie, she..."

"I ran into things I didn't like. And then I ran into a clearance problem, which I never had before. Not with one of my patients, and I don't feel okay about that. And then I thought about you two, and the questions you'd asked, and you'd seemed so *nice*...well, I thought maybe you could help."

"I think we can," Hunter said slowly.

The waitress came back then, smiling brightly. "Can I get y'all some menus?" she asked me and Hunter sweetly, and in just the sort of tone that made me think she didn't actually say y'all ever in her life other than at work.

"We're out of ketchup," I said, smiling. I looked past her and took stock of the rest of the diner. Not a whole lot of people, actually. Nobody was looking at this table of four women. Good. I was starting to get edgy, though. Edgier.

"Sorry about that, I'll go and get you more," she said, and walked off.

I turned to Hunter, who nodded. "Yeah, we can get you out of here like, now if you want. If you think you've got a problem."

"Now?" Beth asked, but Annie was nodding too.

"I think it's best. I know it's a lot, and I don't really know you. I'm really sorry about this. I know I'm asking a lot."

"It's okay," I said, catching Annie's gaze as she started to tip into rambling. She smelled on the edge of panic and that wasn't helping me any. Hunter was...excited, but still in control. If she was like Morgan, she'd always be in control, whether it looked to the rest of us like she'd let a wild dog off the chain or not. "We thought...well, we didn't happen upon you accidentally, let's say that." That was probably too much for me to say. It probably would never matter.

"I don't understand," she said.

"You don't have to," Hunter said. "Beth, do you want the ride or not?"

"I do," she said, no hesitation.

"Then head outside and get in the black Jeep. The driver has hair like Allie's." Beth levered herself up, slowly, and walked out the door. After a few minutes, Hunter stood up, dropped her phone in her jacket pocket. "Allie?"

I stood up too and, still looking at Annie, I said "We'll take care of her. And the babies, when they come. What's your plan?"

"I don't...I don't have one." She shook her head. "I don't know what I thought was going to—" All the glass windows along the front of the diner broke, and a bunch of things chunked onto the diner floor, the walls, and rolled around. Then a hissing noise.

"Shit," Hunter said conversationally, her eyes as big as saucers. She half shoved, half dragged me across the diner to the women's room in the back corner. She shut the door and clicked the tiny door knob lock. Everybody else in the diner was just now starting to yell.

"The window looks big enough," I said, stupidly. My eyes watered, Hunter's too, even as she tore the shade off, shoved up the window, creaking and splintering it in its frame.

She gave a quick look outside, and an audible sniff, though I couldn't smell anything anymore, my nose burning and streaming, my eyes watering. "Clear for now. Can you do this?"

"Right behind you," I said. She was out in the darkness in the next breath, and I boosted myself up to the windowsill, paused. But I couldn't worry about Annie. Did Beth make it to Morgan? Were they both caught?

I dropped the rest of the way to the asphalt and started to run. The fire alarm in the restaurant was braying. I tried to smell Hunter, see her to follow, and then the air parted on one side of me as a bullet went past. I had a moment to think about how a silenced gun didn't sound at all what they sounded like in movies, it sounded different but not at all like—and then a white hot pain punched through the back of my right shoulder and out under my collarbone. I was on my knees and on my face before I could process any of it, just the pain overtaking all of my senses, my vision whited out, my hearing a long high-pitched whine. Hands were on me and I tried to lash out, but then I smelled Morgan and let her drag me half upright by my left arm. I might have screamed when she put me over her shoulder, I didn't know, but I was looking down at the parking lot when my vision fluttered to black.

The next time I opened my eyes, I was lying in the backseat of the Jeep with a seat belt sticking into my back and Hunter hovered over me. Her fake glasses were gone. She had something against my shoulder. The whole right side of my body was burning, and I moved my eyes to see Morgan slap her fingertips against the roll bar as she blasted through a yellow light. "Morgan, you don't believe in luck," I said, a strange rasp in my voice.

She turned her head and looked at me, eyes narrowed and glittering under the street lamps. Her cheeks glistened wet in the light, was she crying? No. I never saw Morgan cry, never. No, they'd used teargas. "Normally I make my own."

"Jesus Christ this hurts." Am I gonna die, I wanted to ask. All I could smell was pepper and blood. So much blood. Was I bleeding that much?

"So hey, why didn't you tell me you were into music?" Morgan asked, facing the road again. I felt like maybe my face was just streaming tears and snot, but I couldn't care. The radio wasn't on. That was weird. "We could do like the Family Von Trapp, have a traveling Culver folk rock gig or something."

"My guitar got all burned up." I thought I told her that before. Yeah, we talked about it before. She bought me a guitar? I thought about trying to sit up, maybe I tried, because Hunter pressed me down again, her jaw set. She moved the cloth or whatever she had against my shoulder and leaned in to inspect the wound, her hair brushing against my face, half out of its bun. She kept sniffing, sniffing, looking for something. Whatever she did made it hurt worse, and a noise caught partway between a squeal and a whimper escaped me. She shook her hand like she'd burned her fingers, and something pinged to the floor.

"What do you know how to play? Don't tell me it's just that church stuff?"

I breathed in, out, in, out, and she looked at me again. She should've been concentrating on driving. I kind of wanted to throw up but thought that would hurt even more. "Is now the time to..." Arguing with Morgan never worked. I tried to concentrate. Morgan never asked me anything. "Landslide."

Morgan laughed, maybe a little too loud. "See, we can work with that. That song's hard."

"What about Howling?" I moved my eyes to Hunter, who appeared to be unwrapping a sanitary napkin. I couldn't really see her face too good.

"Aw, those guys aren't all that serious. Besides, it's all about family." She turned sharply enough that the tires squealed softly. "We can do a Southern Rock metal thing, like Golden Earring." Morgan said something else, and Hunter looked up, and I saw her lips move, but couldn't hear anything anymore. I let my eyes close again.

When I opened my eyes again, nothing hurt anymore. I couldn't feel anything, and the walls were white, and I asked "Am I dead?"

"No such luck," Morgan said from somewhere to my left side, and I turned my head to look at her. She was lounged in an easy chair, legs over one arm, a beer on the end table next to her head.

"What happened?"

"We made it to the Culver family double secret hideaway. As opposed to the first one which was just regular secret."

"Is everybody okay?"

"Other than you, yeah. You thirsty?" I nodded, and she got up and walked out of my field of vision for a moment, then came back with a glass that had a straw in it. The water was cold, so nice and cold. "Sela and Sidney went to the Nortons with the dogs. Frances came here to Florence Nightingale for you. Well no, to doctor you. Florence Nightingale was a nurse."

"What about Annie and Beth?"

"No Annie, but Beth's here." She gave me some more water, then set the glass down and returned to her chair.

"The babies?"

"Don't worry about it."

I felt like I should argue, but my thoughts wouldn't come together; almost everything I reached for just kept getting away, like when you dropped eggshell in the bowl. "How did you do it?"

"Do what?"

"Keep going with a bullet in you, that night we got Rachel back? I've never felt so awful, but you didn't even slow down."

"Oh, that. Remember those adrenaline shots the Wards gave us?" I nodded, and my head felt like a balloon bobbing on a string. I guess Frances brought drugs with her, I couldn't feel my right arm, my shoulder, at all, other than a kind of buzzing heaviness. "Well, I used one."

"I don't think that's how those are supposed to work." I tried to think about if I should have known. Morgan had smelled like blood, but after she killed that guard, it was no wonder. She had smelled like adrenaline, but we all did, and she always was so much more hyped up than everybody else. I should have known.

"No, probably not. But they didn't shoot me with silver either."

"That was silver?" The burning. It wasn't anymore, though.

"Yeah, went through like, the skin and muscle on top of your shoulder, came out the front. Broke your collarbone, did you know that bullet force can do that? It broke up a little, but Hunter pulled out the two pieces she could see with like, makeup tweezers, and Fran thinks that was it."

"I had no idea."

"Also, we're the same blood type. Isn't that lucky?"

"Yeah, lucky." Morgan felt bad, I thought. Though I couldn't really say why. I didn't think feeling guilty was something she was capable of, or else she wouldn't be able to act the way she did. "Won't we all be the same blood type?"

"Hell, I don't know how it works. Maybe we are. Oh, hey, there's also—"

"We'll ask Fran," I said, and slipped off again, though even in my sleep, or haze, I could still tell Morgan was there. That was more comforting than I realized it could be. And I tried to laugh about it, tried to tell her, but I was too far under.

Chapter Thirteen

"Where's the wolf?" I asked the next time I woke up. Morgan was there to my left still, or again, but Rachel was in the room now too.

"He's with Sela and Sidney, and the dogs. They're safe."

"Are we safe?" How had they found us at the diner? They must've followed Annie. They must've known all along, and hoped she would lead them to us. It was a trap. Of course it was a trap. How had Morgan lost them, after? They shot me right there in public. They teargassed a whole diner full of people.

"So far," Rachel said tightly. "Your mother never knew about this place, so probably, yes. That we can tell, nothing was on Beth there that they can track."

"I'm sorry," I said.

"Sweetheart, for what?" Rachel came to my side, picked up my left hand.

"If Mama hadn't—" But I didn't really know where to go.

She gave me a squeeze. She was standing right there and felt a million miles away. "Hush now. You couldn't know. None of us did."

"What're we gonna do?"

"You're going to rest and get better. We're going to figure something out."

"With the Wards?"

Morgan made kind of a snort noise that I couldn't really interpret, and Rachel shot her a look. "Yeah, with the Wards. Maybe."

"Maybe? What's wrong?"

"Bill is still pushing for us to hold up some end of a bargain we never actually made," Morgan said. "Beating out Silvernail benefits everybody, I don't see why we have to—"

"Morgan." For once, just Rachel saying her name was enough. Normally it seemed to egg her on, but everybody just keeps doing it.

"What do they want?"

"Same thing they always do," Morgan grumbled, and Rachel looked at her again.

"I never really thought about babies before, and now I'm tired of everybody wanting ours," I said, and the effort of all of it just wore me out. I closed my eyes, the deep-seated throb starting in my shoulder and collarbone again. I'd never broken a bone before, or been shot, and it was shocking, how much it hurt. How much it all hurt. I'd also never done any kind of drugs before other than drinking some beer, and had no way to know the way they'd make me feel either, drifting from myself like a loosely tied boat.

"Just hush now, Allie," Rachel said. She put my hand down, but stood there for a while. Long enough she thought I was asleep again, I guess. I kind of felt like I was asleep again. I wasn't awake, anyway. "Don't you get her upset," she said to Morgan, quietly, fiercely.

"Me? What am I gonna do to get her upset?" I could imagine Morgan's wide-eyed, innocent act. Except maybe this time it wasn't an act?

"Don't say anything more about the Wards right now. Or about her mama at all."

"I didn't intend on it."

"It won't help anything."

"Rachel, I *know*. Jesus."

"Just making sure. Sometimes..."

"I know I do stupid shit, but come on, I'm not totally out of pocket."

"Good. I'm glad we understand each other."

"I'm not sure I'd go that far," Morgan said, and they both laughed quietly, ruefully. I fell the rest asleep then, before Rachel left the room, before I could make my mouth shape the questions, ask why they were talking about Mama, if something happened. I thought something happened.

Whatever the drugs were, the painkillers, just pushed me under most of the time and I didn't dream. Sometimes I did, a little, just impressions of things. The woods at home, or summertime and a sprinkler, or driving around with Morgan. Fran must've been worried about my dose, though, or probably she had a plan all along, and the next time I woke up I felt more clear headed. Morgan wasn't in the room, for the first time, and I wondered how much sleep she'd been getting, then laughed at myself; how much sleep did Morgan ever get?

I sat up, experimentally. I'd been propped up on a couple of pillows, more than I normally slept on, and my right arm was in a sling against my chest. I thought about it, looking down, and came to the foggy conclusion that it was how the collarbone was taken care of. It wasn't like they could put it in a cast.

What did Rachel mean about Mama, though?

I threw the blanket back, clumsily, left-handed, and swung my feet to the floor. I stayed that way for a while, head hanging again, as the room wibble-wobbled around me and I thought I might just fall over from the effort and the pain flashing like a lit-up sign that had something wrong with it. It steadied enough eventually, though, and I stood up slowly. I couldn't hear anybody, couldn't smell anybody right nearby. The walls were white, but it was a room in an old house, not a hospital. Obviously it wasn't a hospital. Signature Culver rag rugs on the dark wooden floorboards, and I knew how to make one of those birch rocking chairs like was in the corner. I cocked my head, and could just make out Morgan and Rachel talking, probably in the kitchen, because now I could smell coffee too. I heard footsteps but didn't sit back down on the bed before Fran came in the room.

She smiled when she saw me, a lot like Morgan but...well not tamer, exactly, but more used to reining herself back for people. More comfortable with it. Like how Hunter was. "Good to see you're up," she said. "Just don't overdo it like my sister."

"I needed to stretch," I said. "But I'm glad to finally meet you. I've been hearing a lot about doctor Fran."

"I'm sure you get an earful every once in a while," she laughed; she had a scar through one of her eyebrows that I could only wonder so much about, because where else would she have gotten it but Morgan? Then I felt bad for thinking that. "Sit back down for a sec, let me look at you." I did.

"Where are we?" I asked as she undid my sling, and then peeled back my wound dressing. I hadn't really paid attention to what I was wearing, didn't think about where it might've come from, but it seemed like a tank top and then cotton pajama pants. Or scrubs, maybe. I bit my lip when the bandage came away, huffing short breaths through my nose.

"An old house, and I forget just now how it came into the family, so don't ask for the genealogy rundown if you don't mind."

"Yeah, but—" and I caught my breath when she touched the back of my shoulder.

"Sorry." Fran took her hand away, waited, and when my breathing evened she tried again, her fingers feather light. "West Virginia, if that's what you were really asking. Just north of the Virginia border."

I nodded. Closer to Alabama than New Jersey or Pennsylvania. And Mama and Daddy and the boys. But Mama...something happened, I knew it. "Thank you," I said when she stepped back, crossed the room to the dresser, pulled out more gauze, and medical tape.

"You're welcome. It's what the family doctor is for."

"I actually don't know what kind of doctor you are," I said.

"Genetics research, but before I specialized, I did a trauma rotation." Of course.

I thought about asking Frances about Mama. But I didn't. I couldn't find the words anyway, so I just let her dress the wound again, give me some water and pain pills. I had a feeling in my gut, a growing certainty, that something real bad happened down home and that there probably wasn't anything to do about it. And Rachel wasn't going to do anything about it anyway. Rachel was done. Rachel just wanted to hide until they forgot, after they couldn't find us.

I waited for Frances to leave, and half drifted to sleep again when the pills cottonwooled my shoulder, and thought about how I was going to slip out on a houseful of werewolves who were all better at being wolves than me, and go home to see for myself. They'd only want to stop me, I was sure, to tell me that Mama left me with them and it wasn't my life anymore, or my family. That it was Mama's fault we'd lost our insular life in the Pine Barrens, and we should just let things lie. Let her handle her own consequences. But I couldn't do that, and even through the painkillers I felt all jumpy and fidgety, and like I could hear every sound in every corner of the house, every person and every voice, from Bill and Luke Ward in the kitchen to Everett playing some video game to Morgan practicing guitar in her room without plugging it in, her phone vibrating with a text once in a while. Joe turning book pages.

I slept, or thought I slept, and then came awake and aware when the moon was still high but the house was finally quiet. Nobody was in the room with me and I got up slowly. Every step took an eternity, and pulling jeans on was even worse. Trying to take off my shirt, with the idea of putting a bra on was almost enough to put me on the floor with the bullet wound tunneled through my shoulder, and I gave that up pretty much immediately. I stole Morgan's jean jacket from the chair where she'd left it. I didn't bother to find socks. It was lucky my boots were in the room.

It seemed impossible that nobody was going to wake up and stop me. It seemed like I was making such a racket, as I went out into the unfamiliar hall, found the stairs, crept down them. Every hair on my arms stood up, and on the back of my neck, like instead of walking through the dark I was walking through a closetful of wool sweaters and the static was prickling me, and then I found the front door and went out onto a big sweeping porch, a verandah complete with couches and a multitude of sleeping dogs. They looked at me, their eyes flat and green flashing in the moonlight, and I turned my head and yawned and they all looked away again as I went down the steps, freezing on the final creaking one, my eyes wide in the moonlight, my ears straining back to the house. Nothing.

Whose dogs were they? Morgan said the dogs were with Sela and Sidney. Were there really dogs at all, or was I seeing things? I kept thinking I was going to wake up again, in that room, still in bed. I didn't wake up again.

Taking one of the cars in the yard would be too loud, and I started to walk down the wide winding driveway, my toes getting colder and colder on the loose stones, until I thought I was far enough away to stop and put my boots on. I couldn't tie them, and didn't want my clattery laces to bring everybody running. The woods were quiet, and the dogs were quiet, and the house was quiet, and I wondered if I was too drugged to drive and that's why they were letting me try to go. Eventually I was going to tire myself out, and somebody would come carry me back to bed. Laughing about it. But then I got to the main road and stopped, leaning against a tree and panting, and then picked a direction to go.

It seemed impossible that I'd find any cars along this road, and then there was one on the shoulder ahead of me, like a mirage. I looked through the window, and it was a stick shift. If I couldn't change my shirt with my arm like this, no way could I drive stick. I kept walking. There was a lot of light up ahead, like there was a town or a truck stop or something, blooming pale yellow into the big night sky, and when I looked for the moon again, it was down. Did I have a phone with me? I poked at my pockets and found a wadded handful of small bills, a pre-paid credit card, jack knife, and one of the phones, good. Then another car. Why *were* there cars here? Hunters coming out in the middle of the night? Was somebody gonna come running when they heard it start? It both wasn't locked and was an automatic. I leaned under the dash, thankful for Morgan's juvenile delinquent lessons, and fumbled for an eternity with the wires one handed until I had the right ones, then got the connection and the engine coughed alive. Nobody came running as I fumbled to adjust the driver's seat, pulling the door shut. The gas light was on, and I drove towards the lights.

It was a truck stop, and the entrance to a highway that didn't mean anything to me. I'd never been to West Virginia before. After I ran the card, filled the tank, I sat in the car and looked at a map of West Virginia, squinted at where it met Virginia, and then where Virginia met Tennessee, and from there I thought I saw where I had to go to get back home again. It wasn't home anymore, I knew that, but I didn't have a home anymore, just family. And Mama still felt like family in my heart, even though in my head I knew it wasn't quite right.

I drove and drove. The sun came up and the phone buzzed in my pocket and I pretended I was Morgan and ignored it. They were worried or mad or both by now, I was sure. I couldn't reach to turn on the radio and I sang songs to keep awake and focused instead. I hoped I wasn't weaving too much, I didn't have my wallet if I got pulled over and didn't have Morgan's just right way of telling plausible lies to people who couldn't smell to know better. We wolves were probably good at being cops.

Then it was daylight and I was a few hours from home and I definitely couldn't drive anymore, my shoulder roaring to angry, iron-tinted life. I held myself together long enough to go to a drugstore, buy a bottle of baby aspirin. It seemed like Morgan had said never to take something and I couldn't remember if it was Tylenol or ibuprofen so I chose neither and took six of the aspirin, thinking it wouldn't work, it couldn't possibly work. I wasn't on a highway anymore, just the back roads, and I found a park to pull into, following the signs, and sat in the car in the lot with my windows cracked, and shivered and sweated in the pain until it did dull, finally, not enough, not nearly enough, but bearable. I dozed some, and my phone buzzed more, and I still pretended I was Morgan and ignored it. Morgan with my untied boots, going off because I took it in my head that it was something I couldn't not do, no matter what. Then the long silvery purple twilight came, and I woke up, or was still awake, and I took more aspirin and got on the road again.

Chapter Fourteen

S tanding in the driveway, I knew nobody was home. I hunted under the edge of the porch, left handed and awkward, until I came up with the hidden key. It chattered against the lock a few times until I managed to drive it home, and the click of the lock and creak of the door was so sweet and familiar that I had to close my eyes against the rush of memory.

But I could smell the blood and the bleach. And there was nobody home.

I crept through the house, nostrils flared, not turning lights on, staying away from the windows. It seemed like five men, maybe more, had come for Mama and the boys. And Daddy. I didn't know when. Not the day before yesterday, maybe not even within the last couple of days. A week? Two weeks? I didn't know when anything happened, getting shot, waking up, nothing. Three weeks? The whole world changed in three weeks. Or three days, who even knew.

Jason and Kevin, I thought they'd been taken from their beds, and I could smell the sourness of tranquilizers. Maybe they'd shot them with dart guns from the doorways, like wildlife. The boys were their creation, theirs and Mama's, and Silvernail still treated them like animals.

Mama, it seemed, had walked out. Once they had the boys, I was sure she didn't fight at all, but I couldn't tell which happened when. It was in Mama and Daddy's bedroom that there was blood spilled, dried in the cracks of the wooden floor despite the bleach. Daddy's blood. I leaned my head against the splintered door frame, eyes closed, as black spots crossed my vision like moths. The Silvernail people got into the house, and then crept through quiet enough that my human family didn't hear them. They drugged the boys, then kicked Mama and Daddy's door open. When Daddy came up off the bed, they shot him. When Mama went to him, she sank to her knees into the spreading pool of his blood, and then they pulled her up and showed her the sons she'd wanted so much. The normal sons. She left with them, trailing Daddy's blood with her scent. They came back and took Daddy out, washed the place up. Didn't fix the door. Closed and locked the front door.

Rachel had been right about yet another thing. Whatever the reason, Culver love, it didn't last.

Gravel crunched outside, and I raised my head, eyes closed again. I needed my hearing to cooperate. There was a truck outside, maybe two. Not Morgan, or the aunts. Not Wards, or not Wards that I knew. I opened my mouth and sniffed deeply: gun oil and antiseptic. And silver.

Mama and Daddy's room faced the back woods, and Mama always liked having the window open a crack, summer or winter. I slid the window open enough to get out of it, then worked it down again. I could hear their footsteps, still out front. They didn't know who was here, but had a reason to investigate. Maybe just the car I'd left down the block. I was able to think straight enough to park it down the block, not out front. But they hadn't come around back yet. I backed down the roof in a reverse one armed army crawl, reached the edge, dangled my feet, and dropped as lightly as I was able. I would've sworn I felt the broken ends of bone grind against each other, and I froze a moment, listening hard. I wasn't sure I wasn't going to throw up. I wasn't sure I didn't cry out. I gritted my teeth against the pain, the sudden way my head was swooping again. Lord, please don't let me pass out here. Nobody moved faster, or seemed to react. I ran for the edge of the woods on the balls of my feet, pulling the sling off my neck as I ran and shoving it inside my jacket. Morgan's jacket. They didn't have dogs with them and that was a blessing. It was important to count your blessings.

There must not have been any rain or anything for months, the woods were dry, dry, dry. Good for me, hard dirt was hard to leave tracks in. I ran in a whisper with my heart in my teeth, counting in my head how much time had passed, and then picked a tree to go up. My shoulder didn't like it one bit, or my broken collarbone, and my right arm tingled all the way down to my fingertips, but I forced myself through it and I made it up. I could feel the hot blood like sweat start again under the bandages, and everything burned like iron set on a stove, but I got up to a branch I could sit on and wrap my legs around the trunk. I'd never yet climbed a tree in work boots with a shot up shoulder, but I guess I'd managed all right. I felt like throwing up, like screaming, like sobbing, and my eyes were full of static, everything doubling, tripling.

They went through the house; their shadows swept the windows, their grasping flashlight beams. I hated their boots on Mama and Daddy's floor, their eyes seeing our things. Their things. Not mine anymore. Not my house anymore not my life anymore not my family anymore.

I saw the black moths in my vision again and prayed that I wouldn't pass out and fall out of the tree. Then I prayed that I would die, if I did fall. I didn't want to end up in a lab with my head shaved while they drew my blood and shocked me and tried to get me to change on camera. I didn't want to think about who would be watching that. After a long time, a very, very long time, they came out of the back of the house. They weren't trackers, or if they were, they didn't find me because they couldn't smell me. They went back and forth in the backyard, came into the woods a little bit, but seemed to lose interest quick. They swept with their flashlight beams, flashlights mounted on guns whose purpose I could not tell, and then withdrew. I smelled the smoke before I saw the flickers in the house.

Why didn't they burn the house before? Did they leave it as bait for me? They must have.

I thought about using the phone in my pocket. How would I explain myself, though? Anybody I called would recognize my voice, the blessing and curse of a small town. What was the point in saving the house anyway? Daddy was gone. Mama was gone. Jason and Kevin. Plus, as far as that house was concerned, our family had no history. But I was so tired of watching lives burn.

I was too filled up with smoke to smell her, but I heard Morgan come up the path from the other direction, recognized her gait. The fire department was beginning to rouse itself; the distant sirens were growing more sure of themselves. I didn't know how much time had passed. "Are they coming for you or for the house?" Morgan asked softly. I looked down, and saw her eyes gleam in the moonlight.

"I didn't call them."

"Do you need help down?"

"No." Yes. Lord knew I wasn't as invincible as Morgan, but it was better for both of us if I could shimmy my own tail down the tree. How would she even help me? I somehow made it down, and made it before the first fire truck hit the driveway, and we faded back through the woods, towards the high school. "How'd you find me?" I asked. "How'd you catch up to me?"

"Where else were you gonna go?" She didn't see fit to answer the other question. Maybe I slept in the car longer than I thought. I had no reason to believe that my perception of the days was accurate.

The wind changed, and the smoke cleared out of my nose for a minute. I veered to the right, sharp, and Morgan was left to follow me for once. About a hundred feet in, I dropped to my knees next to a patch of ground. I put my hand down, and the dirt was loose. It had been dug recently, and some of the underbrush dragged back over it. Her nose was sharper than mine, so Morgan didn't bother to ask, just stood silently behind me; this was what they'd done with my Daddy after they shot him. I leaned on my left hand and cried as quietly as I could, mouth open, snot and tears running down my face. I thought about curling up on that patch of disturbed earth and just lying there until branches covered both of us. What was I going to do? What were any of us going to do, about people like that? They had enough money and people, they could do whatever they wanted, and we couldn't stop them.

Morgan gave me time, and then nudged me in the ribs with the toe of her boot. "Come on, we gotta go." It wasn't enough time. There wasn't any way to have enough time. I'd used up everything I had, though, and more, and she had to haul me to my feet again, rough and careful at the same time.

"What are we doing now?" She helped me through the woods, towards the high school. I wouldn't ask how she knew the address, knew where the school was. I wouldn't ask her again how she caught up to me, how she got here just in time.

"Still want to get even with Kyle, don't you?"

"What? With *Kyle*? Now?" My shoulder was screaming loud enough to make my ears ring, and my mouth was dry. I almost didn't know what she was talking about. All I could think of was Mama and Daddy. And my brothers. My shoulder. My daddy. The fire.

"Why, you got somewhere else to be?" Morgan's Jeep was parked next to one of the dumpsters, under mulberry trees that turned everything purple when they were in fruit. She opened the passenger door and lifted me in. There was bottled water on the floor, and I started to reach for one and hit my head on the dashboard. I left my forehead pressed there for a minute before she leaned me back against the seat, took the lid off a bottle, and pressed it into my hand.

I drank half the bottle before I could make myself stop. She rattled with a pill bottle, gave me two, and I didn't even ask, just took them, drank more water. "Morgan. My mama. My brothers." My daddy. Though I couldn't say that.

She leaned over me to fasten my seat belt. "I got people on it. Trust me. Anyway. Kyle is a football player?"

I shook my head, trying to concentrate. With the full moon, the field was lit up like for a game. The shadows, though, were very dark. "Yeah. Football."

"That's good, because I already poured out the gas." Morgan shut the door on me, and then went around to the driver's side and got the Jeep started.

"What gas?" I asked, slurring a little. But I realized I could smell it, some noxious mix of gasoline and kerosene out on the football field. It mixed with the smell of cut grass and whatever the lines were painted with. Chalky paint stuff. She walked in front of the Jeep and turned to smile at me for a minute, teeth flashing in the night. Then she struck a match and threw it.

Spidery blue flames licked along the ground away from her, then there was a sound like a hard heavy sigh and the field lit up. She'd used the yard lines like big notebook paper. "Kyle Dodd is a rapist."

Morgan ran to the Jeep, laughing, and got into gear and on the road and only then turned the lights on. "Kind of a blessing they set your house on fire," she remarked. "How many fire trucks has this town got?"

"One? Two? I don't know." I finished the water and tried to put the cap back on, but it all just fell out of my fingers. She'd gotten or stolen the painkillers from Fran, then.

"You think lighting fires is standard operating procedure for Silvernail, or just that one of their operatives is a firebug?"

"I didn't think about it." I tried to think about it. The same person, in the house in the pines. In the house here. Shooting us, putting darts in us. Loading silver because it would hurt us more. "I can't remember any of the smells. If somebody at the pines was at my house. I'm trying."

"Just think about it. It'll come to you."

I didn't quite black out then, but I grayed out. I could feel the Jeep moving still, and hear Morgan singing something softly to herself. Not one of her metal songs, but I didn't know what song it was. I couldn't find the strength to open my eyelids, but I asked "You said somebody's on it. Who's on it?"

"Who's on what?"

"Damn it, Morgan."

"The Wards are. Or will be. I think."

"What does that mean? How did that happen? I thought Rachel was done. She was satisfied her people were covered, and Mama doesn't fall under that particular umbrella any longer. She didn't anyway, but then really not, after what she's done." I didn't think I was making sense and kept talking to try to make more sense.

"No, you're right. Rachel's more than ready to go to ground on this one, she was even before she really grasped the email stuff. Lord knows where we'll go next, at this point."

"So the Wards?"

"I told them I'd be a baby mama."

"Oh, Morgan." I managed to get my eyes open for that. She gave me a sidelong glance and grinned. "So then what?"

"So then Bill Ward was just tickled pink to offer his family's assistance, as he feels Silvernail should have no research fodder whatsoever, or no more anyway. He just needed an excuse, really, though maybe he would've gone on his own after we rode off into the sunset?" She slowed down a moment and looked at her palm. I didn't need to smell the ink to know there were directions there. "We're going to get a motel, and somebody will rendezvous or whatever the fuck and lead us to the next checkpoint. We've got plenty of NATO alphabet camp names left, right?"

"So just like that? Nothing's that easy."

"No, nothing is," she agreed amiably, handing me another bottle. "Drink more water."

"Tell me."

"Well, so then me and Luke were in the back seat of one of the Wardmobiles because it wasn't like I could, uh, shake on that agreement under Rachel's roof what with her having already laid down the law and all and...well, remember how I told you that you can break handcuff chains with a seatbelt?"

"Oh, Morgan."

"Well, I guess Luke didn't know that."

"Morgan you didn't."

"I did. I mean, I did cuff him and leave him alone in the back of that car. I didn't actually want to have sex with Luke. Well. Not right then. The moment wasn't optimal." She looked at me again, until I drank some of the water just to get her eyes back on the road. "Maybe someday. But anyway, I made my departure from the Wardmobile and into my own chariot and then here we are."

"I'm surprised he couldn't just break the handcuffs on his own."

"I am too, and I'm sure he did, but not before I cleared the driveway. I'm really giving credit to the element of surprise, not so much those cheapy handcuffs. Well I guess maybe it was hard getting leverage? I'll have to try it with one of the other pairs."

"Nobody ever knows what you're going to do. Didn't they have safety releases?"

"I mean, yeah, until I broke 'em. And he also may have been somewhat drunk. Seems that when Rachel pulled the plug after our latest debacle, they thought all of us would. For people who are so 'intel oriented', they didn't pay much attention, did they?" She took her hands off the wheel to make the air quotes, and I wondered with interest if I was going to die tonight after all.

"No, I guess not," I said, or tried to say. I was having a hard time forcing words out right.

"Get some rest, Allie," Morgan said, and I grayed out again. This time I was lost in the fog for a very long time, the smell of smoke harsh in my nostrils, the smell of gun oil and boots in Mama's house. None of them were wolves. Did I recognize any of their scents? Maybe I did.

"Why are you being so nice to me?" I asked. I realized the Jeep had stopped, and we were side by side on a dubious motel bed. Morgan had a scratchy washcloth fresh from its laundry shrink wrap pressed against my seeping bullet wound. The TV was the only flickering light in the room, but Morgan had the sound almost off, and I couldn't tell what she was watching from the ringing in my ears.

"We have to watch each other's backs, yeah?" she asked, then cut her eyes back to the TV and I realized she felt guilty. Morgan's conscience was bound to surface sooner or later, I supposed.

"Thank you," I said, and patted her bloodstained hand with my good one. She kept the pressure even, and somehow it didn't hurt.

"Don't mention it," she said. "To anyone." I laughed, and winced, and slipped into a real and deep sleep.

Chapter Fifteen

The next morning, I took a shower on my own, and then Morgan bandaged me up again, helped me get dressed and put my arm back in the sling. "Gotta be careful or you're gonna fuck up your recovery," she said. I thought about the limp she had now from the bullet in her hip, the months of trying to keep her quiet and distracted to allow her time to heal, and I laughed. Maybe if I wasn't on the drugs I was, I'd've been able to keep quiet. "What?"

"You're great at giving advice and terrible at taking it," I said.

"Well. Yeah, I guess so." She grinned but her eyes still looked kind of mad, and I couldn't care. My daddy was dead and buried in our woods. They burned my house down. The house down. We never had dogs; maybe if we had, even just one, Mama and Daddy would've had warning and been able to call sheriff Hagan. The fact that none of this Silvernail stuff has been in the news said to me they didn't want to deal with police, no way, no how. Or, they didn't want to deal with publicity, and were always able to handle the police just fine. That one seemed more likely, and made all of this that much worse.

"So what's the plan?"

She shrugged, sweeping a bunch of medical stuff into a duffle bag. I didn't know if she'd just emptied the dresser from that room I woke up in, or if she actually got Frances to sign off on what we were doing. Maybe a little bit of both. It occurred to me that I never saw the two of them in the same room together, and I thought about that scar through Fran's eyebrow.

"We'll meet up with the Wards, see if they enjoyed my cheeky prank or if it was a deal breaker. They're acting like they're still on, anyway. Maybe Luke just likes 'em spirited. Then, we'll see about your mama and brothers."

"We know how well a facility break did last time, with the Wards," I said, sitting on the edge of the bed.

"Swimmingly," she said, gritting her teeth for a moment. "Let's go."

"You really handcuffed Luke Ward in the back of one of their cars? Did you tell me that?"

"I did tell you that, and I definitely did that." Morgan slung the duffle bag and came to help me up. I'd taken my pills again, painkillers and antibiotics and I don't know what else. Something to counteract the silver, maybe? Or maybe they flushed that out somehow, with alcohol or whatever. "Why are you crying?" Morgan asked me, fastening my seatbelt.

"Everything," I said, after struggling for a minute to try and see what I even wanted to say about it. It seemed impossibly dumb that she was even asking me. Why wouldn't I be crying? "Why don't you ever cry?"

"I guess I just get mad instead," she said.

"So what do you think turns a pharmaceutical company and fertility clinic into militant bogeymen who steal people in broad daylight?"

"Money?"

"I'm sure there are things even you wouldn't do for money."

She frowned. "I'm glad you understand me so well."

"And I might be late to the game here, we all know that, well the Wards don't know that, but *Silvernail*? Like, we Culvers are so into our family histories right? All the begets like the Bible?" Morgan nodded. She kept looking at me sidelong, paying attention to the road thank God but she still had a little frown that I didn't really know what meant. Worry about me again. Still? "Silvernail. That sounds like a made up monster movie werewolf hunter and nobody's talking about that. Did they already talk about that and I missed it? It's just one of those things everybody already knows?"

"Drink some water, Allie," Morgan said, and made the next turn. I picked up a water bottle out of the drink holder and took a couple of sips. When had I last eaten anything? Not like I was hungry. I didn't even know what day it was, or the date. I guess the phone would tell me. I shifted around to try and get it out of my jeans pocket and the pain spiked so bad that I fell back against the seat instead, panting.

"You never said anything about me stealing your jacket," I said when I could talk again. I wasn't wearing it now; she'd brought me another jacket, one I hadn't seen before. Not like I *should* need it, it was summer. But I kept getting the shivers anyway.

"It was right there, it only made sense for you to take it." Did she leave it there for me? Did she assume I was going to run off?

"I guess I should apologize for all the times I acted like your, like I thought you—"

"All the times you turned your nose up at my criminal pro-clivities?" She drawled in a bad imitation of my accent. "Apology accepted. I knew you'd see the light sooner or later."

"Why didn't anybody stop me?" I asked in a very small voice.

She laughed, big and delighted. "Because you were just that good! I didn't want to congratulate you too early, but holy shit. Drugged out of your mind and shot up with silver, you snuck out of a house chock full of goddamn wolves, stole a car, and drove home. I guess you heard me and Rachel?"

"Rachel was telling you not to say anything about Mama, and that it would upset me. That could only mean something bad happened to Mama."

"God, you're an idiot. You're right, but you're an idiot. And I'm proud of you, probably nobody else is gonna say it. Figures it was Rachel's own damn fault."

"I'm glad you taught me how to hotwire a car."

"I'll bet you are. But did coming here make you happy?"

"No." I drank some more water. Morgan once told me that if I ever went home again, Mama would meet me with a shotgun full of silver, and that's not really what happened, though some of the pieces were there. "But come on. Silvernail the werewolf hunter, right?"

"It sounds like the stupidest shit and is probably totally true. Maybe they even followed one of the families from the old country or something, I dunno. Or their great-great-granddaddy ran into werewolves in the Wild West, though I guess one of us wouldn't've been out there to work in any of the mines, right?"

"Or as sheriff," I said with a loopy giggle, thinking of the silver star that got pinned on their chests. Though I guess it probably wasn't real silver. Tin? Tin made more sense probably.

Morgan laughed too, maybe humoring me. "You're right, not a whole lot of us were lawmen. Somebody worked for the Pinkertons, I think. And there's been some U.S. Marshals. Not in our family, though. Plus the military is lousy with Wards, even without Luke in the SEALs anymore."

"How do you know anybody did that, if we mostly keep to ourselves?"

"Well, we keep to ourselves until we don't. And besides, Hunter knows lots of families."

"Because Hunter's a Coutard and Coutards are neutral. But she talks to you about it?"

"Not in enough detail to get a Silvernail kidnap squad on anybody's doorstep, she's a helluva lot smarter than that, but yeah." She paused for a second. "Allie you're crying again." I didn't know what her tone of voice meant. But all I could think of was Daddy's blood and bleach in the house, Daddy in the woods. Mama's picture on the wall of that clinic, smiling with the boys. I kind of sniffled and nodded, my eyes closed. I heard her sigh, and after a couple of minutes, or maybe longer, she pulled the Jeep over, and then leaned over and carefully hugged me, but not even the shock of Morgan being nice and comforting could stop me crying, and I pressed my face into her shoulder and sobbed until my throat was raw and my eyes felt like they were packed with fiberglass. For once, Morgan didn't seem impatient with me, or about to crack a joke. She was angry, but Morgan was almost always angry. I was angry too, when I wasn't sad. When I finished, or when I was still crying but not sobbing anymore, I sat back up, back against the passenger seat.

"I'm sorry," I said.

"For what?" Morgan was looking at me, really looking, and I tried to figure out her expression. Was she trying to figure out how to get me back to Rachel, get me someplace where I couldn't be in the way? Was she trying to figure out if I was going to be a problem in any number of ways, her and Hunter's relationship among them? I wouldn't know even if I wasn't taking the pills she gave me.

"For being an idiot. I don't know." I sniffled again, my breath hitching. "He's just buried in the woods. And we just left him there."

"Probably the sheriff's gonna come through with dogs, after they found the house the way it was," Morgan said. "So what do you think they told anybody about you?"

"What they said about why I was gone? They put it in the paper that I went on mission to Kenya."

"Gross. And they believed it?"

"Daddy was the pastor." To me that once would've meant everything, it was my whole world. To Morgan, I was sure it meant almost nothing. Sure, we had the Culver family Bible, but more as a historical document than something we looked to for comfort or guidance. That's what the Foxfire books were for, or Lydie's daybook, or any number of other concrete things which had to do with what was right in front of us rather than spiritual concerns. And it hadn't bothered me, not really. Some pastor's daughter I ended up being.

I still wore my cross, the steel copy Rachel had made for me of the silver one I'd worn most of my life, but I didn't ever pray anymore, other than the usual last minute kind, the fingers crossed for luck kind, not the sort that really had anything to do with the Lord. And this was the first time I'd really thought about it for what seemed like a very long time, since that night coming back from the school party. Since Mama brought me to the aunts. And now Daddy, if he was in heaven watching down on me, the way we'd always said about people, the way I'd always believed, he'd know how wicked I'd been. And how good I'd tried to be.

"We gotta keep on going," Morgan said after a while. "Are you hungry?"

"No."

"You should eat something." She looked at me again before putting the Jeep back into gear, like she couldn't understand the state of not being hungry. Even after she'd been shot, getting Rachel back, she'd been hungry the next day. She was tougher than me almost all around, no contest. Maybe the silver was why I was so sick. That had to be it.

"Okay."

We didn't go to a sit down restaurant, just stopped at a gas station that had some kind of a no name fast food place attached. Maybe it was a chain once and the franchise got shut down or something, I didn't know, but Morgan gassed up the Jeep and then went in and got us burgers and fries, milkshakes.

"We'll be at the Wards' in another two hours or so," she said.

"I don't remember you talking to them."

"You'd dozed off again. Which reminds me, take your pills."

"You don't need to keep me drugged and docile to get me to go along with whatever you're doing," I said.

"I know that. These are antibiotics. And something else, something to do with the silver. The painkillers are on a different timeline."

"Hey, what was it we're not supposed to have? I got baby aspirin because I didn't bring anything with me."

"Aspirin's okay. We're not dogs, you know." She paused. "I guess maybe we shouldn't buy Silvernail branded stuff though, huh."

"Oh. Oh no." I must've looked really stricken because she kind of patted my knee.

"Okay, okay then, calm down. What was the other thing? We're not dogs. Concentrate on that."

I took a deep breath. "Okay. Uh. Yeah, I know. It doesn't mean I want to eat chocolate anymore, though." I wondered if Mama took that chocolate bar out of her glovebox or if it was still there. Or if one of the boys found it.

Morgan made a face. "Right? It tastes weird."

"Did you ever like chocolate? You got wolfy way earlier than a lot of people, you said."

"I guess I did. Reese's, I liked chocolate and peanut butter. And Ivy's people do that carob thing, which tastes kinda like chocolate. And not so bad, if chocolate doesn't taste good to you anymore."

"I thought we didn't really see Ivy's people."

"I haven't since I was what, eleven? Something like that. So we really don't. But the last time we did, they had carob brownies."

I imagined for a moment a full on Culver family reunion, all the branches together at some big park somewhere, putting food out on the sun bleached picnic tables, the kids all running around in the way kids at those functions did. But then I imagined them all getting together, and after lunch or dinner or whatever, when evening set in and all the regular folks were out of the park, dropping their clothes to the ground and turning into wolves to run through the trees under the starlight. I was certain it's what they did. Did it feel totally normal to me yet? I wasn't sure. It wasn't scary anymore, anyway.

Chapter Sixteen

I t was Tyler and Joe Ward who met us at the rest stop, though they only gave us a nod before we followed them back onto the highway, up a couple of exits, and then off onto a series of roads that led us to another one of their camps. Was this Camp Echo? I'd lost track. Morgan claimed to have never bothered keeping track to begin with, but I didn't know if I believed her. She also told me not to call Rachel, but that I should text her that we were okay, and I did. She told me to turn off my phone again and I did. And it was my phone, now that I looked at it. Morgan left my phone in her jacket. It could only have been on purpose.

We got out of the Jeep, and before I even came around the side of it, Luke had appeared out of nowhere and shoved Morgan into the side of the vehicle, slamming her door closed with her back. "What the fuck?" she yelled, but she knew what the fuck, and I saw that glitter in her eyes.

"We had a deal," Luke said. His face was red, right up to the tips of his ears, the way we'd seen Joe blush. Luke was furious and Luke was embarrassed and I could smell both of those things. Luke was also much bigger and stronger than me even in the best of times.

"We still got a deal, the time just wasn't right," Morgan said, with an infuriating smile. She started to shoulder past him and he shoved her again, rocking the Jeep. "Now, you don't wanna keep doing that." Her voice was calm and just crackled with the heat lightning of a threat. She'd wanted a piece of Luke Ward since we met him.

"Maybe I do," he said.

I couldn't tell how many other Wards were here, and I also couldn't see this going our way, other than that Luke was acting a fool and should back down, except Morgan was just pouring gasoline on the fire. Gasoline on...oh God, she'd really done that to the football field. My vision swam away from me and my knees turned to water, and when whoever caught me, Joe caught me, I smelled him, he jarred my shoulder and I made another terrible noise. As a distraction, I guess it worked, though I couldn't say I planned it.

"She shouldn't be up and about," one of them said, Tyler I thought, I remembered somebody saying Tyler was a medic.

"We make our choices," Morgan said, but I heard that worried undertone in her voice again. Regret.

"I'm sorry," I said. I didn't know how much time had passed; I was in one of the easy chairs in the cabin, Morgan sat next to me. Other people were in the room, other wolves, more in the next room.

"You'd think you wouldn't be so squeamish," Morgan said conversationally, laughing but not laughing. She'd really wanted to fight Luke. Maybe she had; I could smell blood, and it wasn't mine for once.

I opened my eyes and looked at her. Her face was okay. The knuckles on her right hand were scuffed up. "You'll have a hard time touring again if you mess your hands up," I said.

She laughed. "Ain't that the truth."

"You're okay?"

"Yeah, I'm okay. Are *you* okay? I'd think you were faking to keep me from getting in fights, but you got too good at it real fast without any practice."

"Maybe I finally found something I'm good at," I said.

"Aw, Allie," Morgan said, and then Luke came into the room and she stiffened up, lifted her chin and stared right at him.

"I'm sorry," he said slowly, grudgingly. He looked at her, and looked at me, always assessing, but he did seem sorry. I never expected that. I didn't smell Bill here, I wondered who prompted him to apologize. Unless he'd just gotten a dressing down on the phone. Unless he found his own conscience. We had better things to do than hit each other, even if what Morgan did sometimes made her very hittable. He had a bruise coming out on his jaw, three of Morgan's knuckles imprinting there.

"Apology accepted. You might get in these pants yet." Morgan grinned, and his eyes narrowed. Instead of rising to the bait, he turned to me.

"Are you okay?" he asked, another shocker.

"I think so?" He probably meant my shoulder, and I couldn't feel it again, which meant Morgan probably dosed me. He might've meant emotionally, probably everybody here could smell the upset on me as soon as we got out of the Jeep, it was hard to say. I didn't think I was okay emotionally. Not by a long shot. I kept forgetting and coming back to it, like a dog with a bone. I wondered how the wolf was. I could text Sidney to ask. I didn't text Sidney to ask. Morgan said to have my phone off. "What's the plan?" I asked.

"Right now we're figuring out where they took those people," Luke said. "If they took those people. They killed somebody there, for sure, a man. Not sure what they did with the kids. The woman who walked out, she wasn't fighting anybody, and she got in her own car to leave."

Because they had my brothers, I wanted to say. I didn't. Did Morgan, did anybody, explain why we cared about the people in that house in Alabama? I hadn't been there for any of that talk. The house hadn't smelled like me anymore at all, but now that I thought about it, could I even smell myself?

"And then what?" I asked. Why wasn't Morgan asking anything?

"Then we decide if it's something we're going to pursue."

"They killed somebody," I said. It was hard to talk, and every time I thought about my daddy, my thoughts shut down. "And it isn't the first time. Probably Dulcie wasn't even the first time. They could've killed me." How could they not want to pursue? I thought they already agreed to pursue.

"They're a big corporation who hire what amounts to a private military. They're bigger than whoever we meet when we roll up on a facility. They've got more guns than we do, more tech, more money."

"So how do we make them stop?"

"Who are these people to you?" Luke asked me, and I wasn't as good at meeting his eyes as Morgan was. My stomach felt all wobbly still, and I was regretting my cheeseburger and fries.

"They raised me," I said, a dangerous answer but mostly the truth.

Luke squinted a little, looked at me harder. "That's why we didn't know about you," he said.

I nodded. "'Fraid so."

"Well that'll make Bill feel better about the holes in his intel," Luke said, actually laughing. I wasn't used to this Luke, this almost-friendly Luke. What was *happening*?

"It's why we did it," Morgan said. "Wanted to see how hard or easy it was to throw the Wards off the trail." She was lying, of course she was lying, but I couldn't smell it. Maybe Luke couldn't either. I had no business comparing my abilities to his, but his face didn't change, or his scent, or his posture.

"Well you succeeded," Luke said, still kind of laughing. "Bill's need to gather intel has always been a little weird anyway."

"Glad we weren't the only ones who thought so."

Luke shrugged. "It's what he did in the Navy, so I guess it's a hard habit to drop."

"And what did you do in the Navy?" Morgan asked. She already knew that. I already knew that.

"I was a SEAL," Luke said, with a glimmer of a grin. I had no way to gauge how old I thought he was, or how long ago I thought that was. Over twenty five, by Ardith's division a million years ago at that motel. The Wards seemed to age differently, if Bill was the example. Or maybe not, I didn't know how old Bill was. "But we're working on a solution to the problem. Location and strategy."

"Thank you," I said.

"Maybe the time for us all keeping to ourselves is drawing to a close," Luke said. "Everett and some of the other kids think so. Maybe they're right."

"It's worth a shot anyway," Morgan said. "I know the grownups have a hard time getting along."

He looked at her for a moment, and she smiled sweet as pie, and he shook his head. "We may all figure it out yet."

And then he left us to our own devices, which for me, was holding the chair down. Lord knew what Morgan was apt to get up to. But she stuck with me, hardly even fidgeting. I opened my eyes again and looked at her after a while. She was looking off into the middle distance, not bobbing her head and mouthing song lyrics, not texting, nothing. "You okay?" I asked.

She sniffed and looked at me. "Just thinking. I do that every once in a while, contrary to popular belief."

"Honestly, I figured you had a real hard time shutting your thoughts down, and that it was the root of all your problems. Or most of 'em, anyway. Constant thinking, plus no notion of what's right and wrong."

She laughed. "Well look at you, with your deep insights."

"That's me." I sighed, not really meaning to, and to my surprise, Morgan reached over and took my hand for a minute, squeezed it.

"We're doing what we can," she said. I didn't really know what to do with this Morgan, rock steady, who didn't seem as though she were about to cut loose and vandalize something, or fight somebody. Well, she'd already kind of fought somebody. I had a distant thought, that I should be deeply suspicious that she was planning something, but my weariness and sadness were having an intersection and I just couldn't straighten my thoughts to focus on much of anything. After a while, Morgan said "Let's find you a bedroom."

Chapter Seventeen

Nothing happened the next day or the day after that, and Morgan's stir crazy nature did start to manifest in little ways. More snark and sass. Lots of 'go ahead, I dare you' staring. The usual things. Joe wasn't around. Luke was around and wasn't around. Tyler checked in on my collarbone and bullet wound periodically. He didn't say much, but his worry didn't seem out of control. I guess I could've been dying and maybe he wouldn't've been very concerned, who was I to say? He didn't know me. But little by little, the constantly blinding pain was lessening. I didn't think to ask Morgan how much time had passed since the diner until the third day at the Ward camp.

"Like a week and a half," she said.

"*Really?*" I stared at her. I remembered trying to figure it out, if it was one day or three weeks. I'd never lost so much time before. Or any time, really. Maybe once when I was little and I had a fever for days and days, and just shivered under a pile of blankets in July, Mama making her chicken soup with scratch noodles. How old was I when that happened? Was it because I was supposed to be changing into a wolf and instead Mama made me sick with something from a Silvernail doctor? I couldn't trust anything that ever happened to me.

"Allie, why?" I guessed she'd probably said it more than once.

I shook my head. "I just...I didn't know it'd been so long."

"You got somewhere to be?"

"Not exactly. Though when is Beth due?"

Morgan was real quiet for a minute. "She isn't, anymore."

"*What*?" I jerked upright on the couch, and saw stars when my collarbone chomped at me. Morgan started to get up and I waved my other arm at her and tried to catch my breath. "What happened? She got out, she was in the Jeep."

"Teargas causes miscarriages," she said, tight-jawed.

"She was *outside*." I remembered her walking out, before the glass broke. All the windows. All those canisters, rattling around on the floor.

"They used a lot of teargas." I couldn't say why it took me so long to catch up to just how furious Morgan was, but I guess maybe the fact that she was so controlled about it was what threw me off. And that was even scarier, really. *Calculated* anger wasn't typically Morgan's style. I looked at her hands, though, white-knuckled into fists, and I took as deep a breath as I comfortably could and tried to stop freaking out. No babies. Though also that meant Silvernail no longer had any of our cells or anything. But they had Mama, and the boys. They had whatever information they'd gathered on me, because of her.

"So then how were you and Hunter okay?" How okay could I confidently say they'd been? I was the least okay I'd ever been. I remembered the tears on Morgan's face. Did I really think she was crying over me? No. Maybe. For just a split second.

"We weren't pregnant, and we weren't shot, so we just played through the pain."

"We're never all going to be safe," I said. "Not as long as they're hunting us. They did that in *public*. Did you ask them about Silvernail?"

"I mentioned it. I think they got Everett working on it? Maybe not, I'm not sure they see the value in the history of it all."

"Maybe not." We sat with that for a few minutes, the silence thrumming between us. "They don't have dogs here," I said suddenly. I didn't know why or how it had taken me so long to realize. Maybe because I'd been thinking about the wolf. Maybe because that's where at least some of my underlying nervousness stemmed from.

"What? No, they don't." Morgan cocked her head and looked at me. "What's going on. What do you need?"

"I don't know." What a question that was. What did I need to feel like I wasn't going to peel out of my skin? Not change, that wasn't the feeling I was having. Plus, a three legged wolf was probably about as useful as a one armed human. Movies lied, when they said the shoulder was an okay spot to get shot. Every movie lied. I shouldn't be so surprised by any of it at this point.

"Come on," Morgan said. "Get up."

I got up. We'd been lounging outside in camp chairs, though it was overcast. The Wards didn't pay us much mind, just tried to work around us as part of the scenery. "Where are we going?"

"I want to check on the local news. Somewhat local news. A certain locale's local news."

"The news for..." I trailed off, remembering the scent of paint and football field and gasoline.

"I would've showed you sooner, but it seemed like you needed some more time. Maybe now's an awful time, no idea." She shrugged, half smiling. She was proud of her handiwork, and I guess she should've been, pouring gasoline to make big tall letters like that. I guess she did it by smell more than sight, out there in the dark before coming to get me. How did she know how much gas it would take? How did she know how long I would take? Questions I could never ask, answers Morgan would never think to give me.

"Well thanks," We went inside, to one of the 'command center' areas, and Everett glanced up at us, and pointed at one of the vacant laptops. Morgan must've talked to him about this already.

Morgan put me in the chair, and then leaned over to the keyboard and rattled at it for a second. My town's newspaper was the first result, with a picture of the football field still on fire, though burned down a little from when Morgan had first done it. They hadn't been far behind us. None of the reports we clicked through related anybody fleeing from the scene of the crime, at least. But more important than the field and the fire was that girls I knew, girls from the school, had begun to come forward. Not all of them wanted their names printed, though the case was building that Kyle was, in fact, a rapist. Not everybody had been so lucky as me, to have a pharmaceutically suppressed werewolf heritage, so they could fight back enough to stop him. Nobody should have had to stop him.

"You're crying again," Morgan said, and there was actually a little frown line between her eyes. She was so baffled by emotions. So impatient about everything.

"I just feel so bad for the other girls and so relieved that I am who I am."

"So being a hillbilly freak ain't so bad when it suits you," she said, her grin resurfacing.

"I guess it's beginning to suit me more and more," I said.

"I always had such hopes for you!" she said, starting to clap me on the shoulder and then stopping herself just in time, as I flinched and ducked my head. "Come on, we'll let them do their super-secret intelligence gathering," Morgan said. "And they've got a kitchen that's full of food all the time. You've gotta be hungry by now."

"I guess," I said. I should've been, probably, but didn't feel like food one way or the other. Probably the medication.

"So I think a step three is in order, what do you think?" Morgan asked from inside of the fridge.

"A...step three?" I asked.

She brought an armful of stuff to the table where I sat, mayonnaise, lunch meat, and a loaf of bread. "For the football player. Step one you took care of in the first place. Step two we just saw some reports on. And step three."

"Oh I don't know," I said. I wasn't sure I ever wanted to go back there, with Daddy gone. I hadn't ever thought I would go back to begin with, once Mama dropped me off with the aunts. Once they explained Mama's fear to me. Now I knew what had made her just so religious, why we weren't allowed to have Halloween even. She'd grown up with what she thought were monsters, she didn't want her kids pretending to be them too. Though surprise, Mama, I'm a monster after all. Getting good at it, maybe.

"Scumbags like that, they need a certain flavor of comeuppance, or else they can still always blame somebody else for their own decisions. We'll think of something. Or I'll think of something and you won't have to worry about getting your hands dirty." From the look on her face, she couldn't understand why I wouldn't want to just climb into his bedroom window and tear his throat out. Lure him out to the woods and break every bone in his body.

"Morgan, you never..." I trailed off as she shook her head, turned and got plates and knives.

"No, I never. But it doesn't mean I haven't known people. Rock stars and roadies and things aren't always safe for girls to be around." She paused for longer than I expected. "Whether you're a girl like me or not."

"Until you let me meet Hunter, I never knew any other girls like you," I said, watching her make a number of ham and cheese sandwiches. I couldn't tell if she was making a lot of sandwiches or if I was just so out of it that it looked like she was.

"There's more of us. Wolves and not, of course," she said, and pushed a sandwich at me. "But anyway, it'll be coming up time to bring the wolf to the sanctuary. Though we'll have to be always on the ready, if they find out where your mama and the boys are, the Wards're gonna want to move before Silvernail can do anything about it. We're hoping for a nice clean extraction like when we got Sela."

Morgan almost never stayed on the same thought for long enough. I was getting tired again. I was already tired. "I'm trying to decide if Mama's just bait."

"She probably is. But think of it this way, Annie and the surrogate probably were too. Annie just didn't know it. It's probably a wonder that security let you leave after the interview, they have to know everything that's being sent on the company emails, right?"

"That's true." Morgan was working through her sandwiches very quickly. I took a bite of mine, chewed thoughtfully. No, still not hungry. "So have you checked that email? Did anybody?"

"What, the one Annie used to contact us?"

"Yeah."

"I didn't think of it until now. I guess maybe Hunter did, but she hasn't texted me. Why?"

"If they're using Annie to use Mama as bait..." I guess there was a lot going on, the emails were kind of the least of anybody's worries.

"Allie, you're a genius when you want to be." Morgan grabbed her last sandwich and went back down the hall to the computer room.

"...thanks?" I looked at the sandwich, tried to care about taking the next bite. It didn't really taste or smell like anything, but I thought that was my problem, not the sandwich's fault. It seemed like it was going to stay down, anyway. Morgan had left the sandwich stuff all over the table and slowly, one handed, I started to pick it all up. I felt like cleaning up more than I felt like eating. I smelled Joe as he came down the hall, at least, so he didn't startle me. It seemed like he was maybe walking too loud on purpose.

"I can't believe somebody left you here to clean that up. Sit down, I'll do it."

"It was Morgan, you definitely believe it," I said, but was happy to sit back down again. "Thank you."

"I think we're grilling for dinner soon, anyway," he said, like now that he was in the room with me, he wasn't sure what to talk about. I wasn't either. The Wards sure did like grilling.

"Is it that late?" With the day overcast and how much sleeping I'd been doing, I had no way to tell. My inner clock, which had gotten pretty good, was all confused.

"Yeah, but don't worry about it," he said. He was trying not to look at me too much, I could tell. I wondered if I looked as much of a wreck as I felt. I didn't remember touching my hair today.

"Honestly, I don't even know what day it is," I said, shaking my head, even though that was a pretty big mistake, with how unsteady I felt.

He paused with the fridge door still open. "Well geeze, I don't either, let me think. No, it's Friday, because grandma called over to say somebody better be home to take her to church day after tomorrow."

"Bill isn't home?" I asked. As far as I knew, Bill wasn't here either.

"Bill's still with Rachel, and Ardith Coutard. They're trying to hammer out information exchange, and maybe a more calm and concrete way to deal with our problems on a larger scale. Unless things go down before they get done. Rachel's totally fine on an armistice, she wasn't ever interested in feuding with us anyway, but doesn't want to go after Silvernail at all, no way, no how. She's done, she wants to cut your losses. She figures if we can all stay off the radar long enough, their projects regarding us will just die on the vine."

"I hoped about that. But it also seems like a big investment for people like that to just give up on." Especially if at least one of them really liked hurting us. And burning things down. "But Morgan said that Rachel called everything off."

"They've been too used to getting their own way, right? It seems like it would be too good to be true, if they just gave up now."

"Is that why we're just waiting around here? Because of peace talks?"

"Part of it, I guess. Though I don't expect you're going to be sharpshooting for us again anytime soon." Joe closed the fridge.

"I guess not," I said. It was strangely disappointing, actually. We were trying to stage another daring rescue, and I was going to be sidelined. Not like I wanted to shoot a person, or a dog. Or get shot again. "I didn't really think about that. I don't want to be left behind." Though what was worse, I thought, a pack of strangers getting Mama from wherever, or her daughter turned monster? Or, what was worse, me alone with a bunch of Wards while Morgan goes out and saves the day?

"It'd only be to keep you safe, Allie," Joe said, his voice a new kind of quiet. When I looked up at him to see what it was he meant, he kissed me.

He was gentle, and careful, he didn't put his arms around me or lean in too hard, and risk hurting me. He felt warm, and nice, but it was also the last thing I wanted and I stood up, knocking my chair over, my heart hammering suddenly in my ears. He smelled like meadow grass in the sunshine and wolf. He couldn't possibly have known it was the worst thing to do. I also couldn't find the words to explain it, as his eyes grew sad and his face fell. If I'd thought about wanting any of them to kiss me, I guess it would've been Joe.

"I'm sorry," he said, and turned without looking, running full tilt into Morgan. He actually curled his lip at her, just a little, and then shoved past and out of the kitchen. She looked excited, but really Morgan always looked either bored or excited, and then I thought oh god, the look on my face, and I turned away to the counter, where the coffee pot stood, and I grabbed a mug and poured. I hadn't had coffee in I didn't know how long. Not since before I got shot.

"What was his problem?" Morgan asked, laughing. I shook my head and took a sip of the coffee, and spit it back in the mug. It tasted like it had been heating and reheating in that pot since yesterday, if not longer. It was impossible for it to have been this morning's coffee. "Allie, are you okay?"

Everybody kept asking me that. Even Morgan, which made it that much more surreal. No, I was not okay. I had no way to be okay. "Not really," I said.

"Sit down, you look like you're gonna fall over." I nodded, I kept forgetting not to nod, and she came to the counter to get me and walk me the couple steps to the nearest chair. She took the coffee mug from my shaking hand and set it down, and then her eyes narrowed. "What did that boy do?" she asked sharply, too loud. Suddenly thrilled that maybe she found a fight to distract herself with.

"Shh, shh, nothing, it's fine."

"You're such a shitty liar."

"No, it's okay. He couldn't have known. All he did was kiss me."

"Did he ask first?"

"If he could kiss me? No." There was a thought. "Have you made guys ask you, before they kissed you?"

"Not in so many words, I guess." She picked up the chair I knocked over, sat across from me. Something was scrawled up her arm, but I couldn't read it from here. "But there's been a mutual understanding."

"Well, see then," I said, like that meant anything either.

"I'm just sorry your first kiss wasn't special," she said. I looked at her, and it was impossible to believe that she was serious, not being sarcastic, not ready to laugh at any second.

"Who says that was my first kiss?" I mumbled. Of course it was my first kiss, I didn't need to say that for Morgan to know it was true. She waved her hands impatiently.

"Your first kiss with Joe, then."

"Who says I'm gonna kiss him again?" I asked, and that time her laugh did burst free.

"Atta girl." She paused, like maybe she was going to say more on the topic, and I prayed she'd reconsider, stop teasing me about kissing on the heels of asking what to do about my attacker. "But anyway, you were right, Annie did email us and she is absolutely bait. Bait again? Or she's the hook and this time your mama is bait. They didn't expect us to get away with Beth."

"How did we get away with Beth? I'm a little hazy on that." Due to the unconsciousness, of course.

"Well, it took some fancy driving," Morgan said, proud of herself again, and I remembered the whine of her tires on the road. "And they keep underestimating us."

"That's gonna stop happening pretty soon," I said. "What did Annie say?"

"She said that we could come meet her at the same clinic, where you first came, and that arrangements could be made."

"We can't trust that, though," I said.

"Not the slightest little bit."

"We're not going to go there," I said, like anybody would listen to me if I really put my foot down.

"No, of course not."

"What arrangements would they mean, do you think?"

"Who knows? They want live specimens. They wouldn't've cremated Dulcie if she was of any use to them dead."

"They took samples, the files said. Did a full autopsy."

"They did, yeah. And to most appearances, Dulcie was a perfectly normal woman. And the only reason they didn't test Rachel more was the state they had her in. And then everything they didn't have saved to their network burned up."

"Morgan, what're we gonna do?"

"Well, they're firing up the barbecues for dinner," she said, and looked absolutely astonished when I burst into tears.

Chapter Eighteen

They fired up the grill and did up burgers and sausages, nothing fancy, just shocking in the amount they made. Or maybe not, I should've learned by now. We were all always hungry, except me. Buckets of potato salad and macaroni salad. Ears of corn tossed on the grill. They did up a meal good, even when it was simple.

"Have you heard from Rachel?" I asked Morgan at one point. Joe normally sat with us when we ate, but I hadn't seen him since the kiss in the kitchen. I needed to explain to him what my problem was, and that it wasn't him. I didn't have the energy to hunt him up, and I was too scared to have Morgan do it, but how long was I going to feel this bad?

"No, and for once I want to." She laughed. "Serves me right, right? I'm not gonna give her the satisfaction of calling her, though. She'll let us know when the time comes. Or one of them will. Or Hunter will."

"Do Hunter and Ardith…"

"Get along better than me and Rachel? They get along a whole lot better than Fran and I do. They're sisters, so there isn't the mother daughter thing. But they're sisters, and that's its own can of worms, but I don't think they've gotten in a fist fight since they were little. Which reminds me, Dr. Fran would probably like you to take your meds now." She stood up and her phone rang. She looked at it.

"Rachel?" I asked, and she nodded.

"Hey, Mama," she said when she answered, winking at me. "We're still in Alabama. Camp, I dunno what, Allie do you remember? Is this Echo? Marshmallow? Concertina?"

I laughed. "I think you said Echo."

"Echo, Allie thinks too." She listened a minute. She had her volume fixed so it was low enough I couldn't hear Rachel's voice. Or maybe my ears were still messed up, like how my nose was. "Silvernail burned that house," she said finally, quirked her lips and listened some more. "Well yeah I burned that into the football field. You think staying shut up about a thing like that was gonna do anybody any good? I might be ashamed of you, Rachel." Her tone was easy, joking with an edge as it always was, but the edge sharpened at the end of things and I saw that hard glitter in her eyes again. And maybe I was disappointed in Rachel too. When Mama dropped me off with them, I just had so much happening all at once, I didn't know what I needed for any of it. I still didn't, not really, but maybe being able to, encouraged to, talk about what almost-happened would've helped. Instead they paved it over with the werewolf business and hoped I'd forget. "No, I don't think we're coming home just yet," Morgan was suddenly saying, looking at me.

"Where is home?" I muttered. Now I'd had two homes burn, in two different states even.

Morgan kind of rolled her eyes, but she was tense, more serious. "Rachel, we aren't just gonna let this go. Allie can't. You gotta know that Allie can't." Jaw set, she listened again. "I'm sure you worked out all kinds of great things on paper but that isn't exactly reality. I don't know. I don't—Rachel, I don't know." And she hung up.

"She wants me to just let it go? She just wants us to leave Mama and the boys with those people?"

"They're pretty sure Silvernail won't hurt any of their former experiments," Morgan said, a little grimly.

"While probably *true* that doesn't make it *right.*" I was a former experiment, I couldn't make myself say. And they shot me. With silver. They hurt me on purpose because they'd prefer killing me to letting me get away again.

"What happened to your Daddy aside, it seems your Mama went with them willingly. And will stay with them willingly. Rachel wants you to think about your priorities, think about this family, and think about that wolf that you took possession of before you went running off to do this stuff."

"I didn't exactly plan on any of this." Not one single bit of it from the start up to now. From Kyle and being a werewolf right on up to being shot in a no name diner parking lot and stealing a car to go home again. Shot with *silver,* my thoughts kept shrilling. "And just because they have those experiments in hand doesn't mean they're gonna stop. They did the diner in *public.* That wasn't just finding a house in the pines that nobody knew about and—"

"Shh, I know, Allie. I fucking know all of that already, and that's why I told Rachel we're not—"

"Luke just got off the phone with Grandpa," Joe said from behind us, and I about jumped out of my skin. I hadn't realized how near he was, or how close to crying again I was. "Sorry," he said sheepishly.

"It's okay," I said, wiping my eyes. Morgan looked at him, flicked her eyes to me, looked at him again. I didn't know how much he'd heard either. It wasn't a surprise that he'd snuck up on me, but it was just unbelievable if he'd snuck up on Morgan too. I couldn't tell. I was too upset and hurt to know anything.

"And we just got off the phone with Rachel," Morgan said. The three of us didn't say anything for a minute. I wondered how young the Wards were when they changed. I wondered how Joe was going to end up, with clear expectations that he enlist or something, not wanting to do that. What had the Culvers expected of their daughters? Maybe Fran was the only successful one out of any of us, Morgan's niche fame notwithstanding. What were Coutards expected to grow up to be? They were like U.N. ambassadors or something. Peacekeepers. They were rich, maybe they didn't have expectations in the same way as the rest of us.

"So they all agreed we shouldn't really do anything," Joe finally said. "Unless we want to get the kids, to follow along the lines of messing up Silvernail research."

"Rachel didn't say that," Morgan said.

Joe scratched the back of his neck. "Well and neither did Ardith, I'm sure, but it's what Grandpa put forth."

"Allie?" Morgan asked. I stared at her for a minute. I kinda expected that to be that. If we kept on going, it would be with Ward support, based on her promise. If I understood everything I'd been told, and granted, that could be a little shaky at times with all this interplay. Did she really want to do that? And would she, for *me*? Or did she just want to make sure this bridge was good and burned as burned could be.

"I hate the idea of leaving them," I said. Carefully, I couldn't call them my brothers. Couldn't call her my Mama. Or did it even matter anymore? Probably the less I talked to anybody but

Morgan, the better. Probably the less I talked to Morgan right now, the better. "We don't know where they are yet, do we?"

"Well, no, Everett and the techies are working on that, so a location is only a matter of time, I guess. Even if they pull the plug now, we probably got enough that we can look through everything and match it up."

"Those tech boys, I could just kiss them," Morgan said, with a wicked smile. The tips of Joe's ears went a little bit red, and he dropped his gaze.

"I'm sure somebody'd take you up on that," he mumbled.

"I think Luke's still first in line, yeah?" she asked, and then laughed. Joe laughed too, then stopped himself and looked over his shoulder.

"I guess so," he said. "Maybe not."

"He's completely smitten with me, I just know it," she said, and then winked at me, just slightly. "That's what all the door bullshit was about. We can hardly keep our hands off of each other. We're the ones who're going to bring our families together."

Joe cleared his throat. "But anyway we also aren't going to stay here much longer. Best to move along rather than stay anywhere in force."

"Oh, on to Camp Trident?" Morgan asked, grinning. Joe frowned, looked from her to me. I started to shrug, winced.

"I, uh, don't know yet. Where any of us are going. You two are staying together, obviously."

"Obviously." Morgan just kept staring at Joe, and he kept glancing at her and looking away. He wasn't looking at me at all. "And then what are we doing?"

"We're still in the holding pattern, unfortunately, but I guess it's up to Grandpa at this point? If Rachel says it's off?"

"Like your grandfather was ever gonna listen to Rachel," Morgan said. "No matter what he said at a sitdown." I wondered if she was going to try and pick a fight with him. It seemed unlikely that Joe would swing first, unlike Luke when we got here.

"I didn't think you were listening to Rachel either," Joe said.

"Well no, not really. We do have an errand we need to run, though."

"The wolf?" he asked.

"The wolf," Morgan said, like he'd been her burden, not mine.

"What do we have to do, when we bring him?" I asked suddenly.

Morgan shrugged. "We already did the application and sent over the medical records we had and all that, so nothing. Just bring him."

"Does that seem normal? Is this a good place we're bringing him?" I couldn't stop the plaintive tone in my voice, even though I heard it. I couldn't ignore the little frown on Joe's face, or on Morgan's.

"He'll be okay, Allie. Everett made sure it didn't have anything to do with Silvernail. No research, nothing like that. Just a place for wolves who can't go into the wild because people had them for so long," Joe said.

"Thank you," I said. "Hey Morgan, can we have a minute?"

"Yeah, I guess." She looked at Joe for a little too long before she got up and went outside, maybe to antagonize Luke over something. I didn't have the energy to be worried about this many things at once.

Once it seemed like she was out of earshot, I turned back to Joe, who had an agonized look on his face. "Look, Allie, I'm sorry. I misjudged and—"

"Stop." I didn't really plan what I was going to say, and maybe I should have, with how fuzzy my thoughts were. "You didn't do anything wrong. Your timing was wrong, but you couldn't know that." His expression hadn't really improved. "I'm not doing this right."

"You don't need to make up any reason for how you reacted, I know that I—"

"I'm not making anything up, I'm just not making sense. Just listen to me for a second." I stopped, took a breath. He waited. "Not very long before Silvernail took the aunts, something happened to me. Only they knew, and Morgan. There was a boy and he...well he tried..." I couldn't make myself say it. Even after Morgan spelled it out in big burning letters on a football field. "I hurt him enough to get away. And I haven't really. Processed things, I guess you'd say."

"I'm sorry," Joe said again, but different. Sorry for what happened to me. Worried.

"You had no way to know. So the way I reacted isn't because I don't like you, it's because even without everything else, I just don't know how to handle that right now." There, that seemed like a coherent thought. Joe wasn't making that awful face anymore. "So what I'm saying is, maybe when some of this settles down, maybe enough will have settled in me, too." And maybe one day I could be honest with him about the rest of it too. That would be nice.

Joe took a deep breath, let it out slowly. "That's a lot. You've been through a lot."

"I kind of keep trying not to really think about it. And also haven't really had the time." I laughed a little, and he did too, cautiously.

"No, not really." We sat there in quiet for a couple of minutes, and this time, I waited on him. "Thank you for telling me," he finally said. "I really thought it was because I'm trans."

"You're welcome. And I know, and I really didn't want you thinking that, but I couldn't get my thoughts sorted fast enough to say. So I'm sorry too."

"God, you don't have anything to be sorry about."

"Still." We kind of laughed, having run out of clumsy words. Morgan came back then, which meant either she didn't go very far in the first place, or she really did set some kind of timer.

"Alright, I guess you and me and Joe are going to go to some random Ward's house, spend the night, and then move on to another undisclosed location."

"Not Everett?" Joe asked.

"Oh yeah I guess him too. What a good little team we are. Or, you two have already been contaminated by us and they don't want to risk anybody else." She laughed before Joe or I could react. "Nobody said that, I'm reading between the lines, let's go. How much time do you need to pack?"

"I don't really unpack when we're places like this."

"Perfect, I'll go bully Everett. I wanna get this show on the road."

Everett, trailing past with another techie whose name I didn't know, bristled and came over. "Look, just because I like your band doesn't mean you can talk to me however you want."

"Oh, it has nothing to do with the band." Morgan grinned, kind of tilted her head at me like it was my line, and I grasped for something to add.

"Yeah, it's true. She talks to everybody like this."

"It's what makes it so easy for me to keep my stories straight."

"Most people don't juggle quite so many of them," Joe remarked, but he seemed far less put out than Everett.

"It's a gift."

"It's something," Everett said, shaking his head.

"Does that mean you won't be ready soon?"

"Just give me a half hour or something," he grumbled, and walked off before Morgan could continue her campaign of harassment. Some of it was for my benefit, I thought, to make me laugh at her audacity. Some of it was showboating for the Wards. And some of it was that she couldn't stand to stay still as long as we already had. Maybe that was a gift too; if things kept happening, there wasn't any time to stop and reflect on what had already happened.

Chapter Nineteen

It was starting to feel pretty natural, being on the lam with Morgan, Wards in the back seat, Howling and various associates on the radio. Everett occasionally gave a turning direction to Morgan, and mostly I concentrated on dozing and not getting sick with how the Jeep jounced my collarbone. Everybody could tell I was just keeping myself quiet, I was sure, but somehow they had the decency to let me pretend. At least the night was nice and we had the top down on the Jeep and my pain sweat wasn't just staying clammy on my skin, but getting taken away by the breeze.

"Are we gonna talk about how you two were ready to sneak off behind our backs?" Morgan asked at one point.

"Were we?" Everett asked, seeming genuinely confused.

"I mean, it's like a million years ago now, but back at the cabin. Before—"

"Oh, that," Joe said. "We were hoping to have more information gathered by the time you and Allie got back from your run. So that maybe you wouldn't bite our heads off or something."

"Truly I'm touched. Me and Rachel had you that worried?"

"Sure did." Everett grinned, but not in a happy way. I laughed, surprising myself. Sure, Morgan and Rachel were scary, but Rachel never gave me a beating, never slapped me, nothing like that. Mama was real ready with her hands. I just didn't realize until now that Rachel was never going to hit me in anger.

"Allie, come back to us," Morgan was saying, sing-songing. I didn't know how long she'd been saying it, her voice jokey for the Wards, that frown line between her eyes again.

"Sorry, just thinking," I said. Why did I want Mama back so bad, after all that? Why did I want her to have the boys and be free? Well she hadn't treated them like that, anyway. I wanted to think it was less caring about her, and more caring about preventing her from more betrayal, but the way I felt all twisted up about it told me otherwise.

"It's dangerous when you do that," Morgan said.

"Oh yeah?"

"Yeah. It's when you do things like break truck windshields and start fights in parking lots."

"Morgan Culver, that was you and you know it!" I said shrilly, and Morgan laughed, Joe and Everett cautiously echoing her.

"Yeah, but they didn't."

"You can't convince me that that's true. Nobody in the whole world would believe that was my idea."

"We did already know," Joe said.

"Well it's a better story if it's Allie," Morgan says. "I was just trying it on. There's no way to know how any of this is going to get remembered down the road, you know?"

"Absolutely nobody would believe you that it was me," I said again. "Nobody."

"Allie's right," Everett said helpfully. "Once you both open your mouth, there's no confusing who would've done such a thing."

"Well damn, Allie, they've got us all figured out," Morgan said, in a voice that said they didn't have anything figured out at all.

"More's the pity."

Where we ended up was another nice suburban house, not Camp Trident, which wouldn't have been called that anyway. It was early enough in the day that there were kids scrambling for a bus, but it seemed like a vacation bible school bus, not a regular school year bus. I'd lost track of days, but maybe not *that* bad. Like every other Ward household, they had a lot of kids, five boys, the oldest not quite high school age, the youngest maybe second grade, sports stuff and car toys and buckets of sidewalk chalk somehow involved with the preparations to get them out the door to the bus.

Luke Ward was also here, something that surprised me, and Morgan shot me a quick glance that I couldn't begin to read. Maybe there was just no telling what Luke would do, much like my dear cousin. Or maybe he really was starting to carry a torch like Morgan said. Was that funny? Was that bad? I couldn't tell. I guess maybe Luke hadn't thought about kid logistics either, judging from the look on his face at the controlled chaos we arrived to, and a snicker escaped me before we got out of the Jeep.

Morgan was amused by the fuss, of course, but also corralled me to an out of the way spot on the couch in the living room. A wail came out of the littlest kid right at that crucial moment on the threshold, and the oldest kid said "It was an *accident*!" and fled as the angry mom came stomping out of the kitchen and collared the middle boy. I didn't see what happened, but I had two little brothers. Whatever happened, it wasn't an accident. The woman glared at Luke, who stood talking with the ostensible man of the house, glared at the ostensible man of the house, who'd let us slip past, and started to march the kids into the living room, each held up by the arm and struggling like fish on a line. She stopped short when she saw me and Morgan, looked at her husband again.

"What are we doing here, Rich?" she asked him.

"Send them to the bus, Gina," he said.

"But he—" the littlest kid started to say.

"Justin, you shut your mouth, get your backpack, and get on that school bus," Gina said. She released both kids, and the middle one helped his little brother get his bag and his chalk and get out the door.

"Sorry to drop in on you like this, Gina," Luke said. Morgan grinned and rolled her eyes at me. She loved seeing this chink in the Ward's organizational armor, this indication that they weren't the paramilitary organization they'd love for us to believe.

"I'm sure you are, Luke. Now don't go thinking you're going to be camping on the back lawn and playing war games 'til August, that just isn't going to happen."

"No ma'am, we're just here for a brief visit. Overnight, if it isn't too much trouble."

"You couldn't have called ahead?"

"I don't know what we were thinking, we should have." Joe and Everett slunk into the living room as well, took their places on the couch. Gina glared at them too, and then looked at me and Morgan again.

"Yes you should have. It's one thing to be family and show up on our doorstep, it's another thing entirely to bring strangers! Who are these girls?"

"They're Culver girls," Luke said.

"Like that means anything." She looked at us. "Who are you girls?"

"I'm Morgan and this is my cousin Allie. Culver, like Luke said. I'm the lead singer for the band Howling, and she's training to be a roadie, except she's really bad at it on account of the broken collarbone. But Howling isn't really touring right now anyway, so she's got time to shape up and learn some things."

"Howling," Gina said slowly. Luke had a look on his face that I couldn't read, if he was irritated or thought this was funny.

"Yeah, it's a metal band. Hard rock, anyway. Genre-defying. Maybe not your thing, but that's hard to tell lookin' at a person. Though actually maybe one of your sons is a fan, I think I recognized his t-shirt. The biggest one."

Gina looked back to her husband, stared at him for a long minute without saying anything, and went upstairs.

"Well that went well," Rich said with a forced smile.

"You Wards really like your domineering women," Morgan said, and Everett barked a laugh. Luke did a slow enough blink that I thought for a second that he'd just closed his eyes. I didn't look at Joe to see if his ears had gone pink again.

"Morgan," I said, then stopped, because what could I possibly say?

"What? It's not like they can't possibly know. And it's not like Gina there isn't keyed in to what's going on, at least a little bit. Or she should be, with how old the oldest boy is getting."

"She knows," Rich said. I wondered what the protocol was, for Ward brides being informed of the family nature. Obviously, they could only tell people that they absolutely trusted, but how had so many men found so many women that they could trust like that? And it had to be before they were actually married, right? Otherwise, what a mean trick that would be.

Morgan kept grinning. "Well good. Now what's the plan?"

"If this is a problem, we'll go someplace else," Luke said. "We thought you'd—"

"No, no, Gina just needs some time, it's okay. No, this is great, it's good to see you."

Morgan snickered. "Time for what, to make up some beds for us? She's gotta be real happy, five extra people, two of them strangers."

"Morgan," I said again.

"But she only knows about the Wards," Morgan said. "Not the Culvers or the other families. Not the feud. Am I right?"

"Yes, you're right. Jesus she's pushy." Rich turned back to Luke.

"She's bored. When she's bored she gets destructive, and sometimes that means socially," I said, before Luke could comment. Morgan gave me a shove, hard enough to hurt and make me stifle a whimper, but not as hard as she could.

"Gimme something to hit, and I'll do that," she said. "Somebody from Silvernail is most preferable, for obvious reasons."

"*That's* what this is about," Rich said, snapping his fingers.

"You haven't been reading the emails?" Everett asked. I didn't think he'd even been paying attention.

Morgan positively guffawed. "Emails?" she asked. Crowed, maybe. "Are you kidding me? You what, have a big email list of all the goings-on? Maybe a family message board? Facebook group? Do you post pictures and the kids' trophies and stuff? The emails, Jesus Christ."

Luke's jaw tightened, and Everett looked like he had a mouthful of sawdust. Joe looked at me, and Morgan let loose again, and I couldn't help myself and started laughing too, even though it shook my collarbone and hurt. It was all so ridiculous, with their special alphabet named places, with Bill Ward's ALPHA license place, with everybody all ex-military or current military, and here was Rich in Kentucky or Alabama or wherever the hell we were and he hadn't kept up on the emails and didn't know we were in a…whatever it was, shadow war? With a Big Pharma bogeyman. Just living his life with his domineering wife and his five boys, with the oldest boy on his way to being a wolf. I wondered what they even called it. I was sure that varied by family too.

I asked, "Okay, so we're here tonight but then what?"

"We're kind of in a holding pattern," Luke said.

"We're narrowing the locations," Everett said. "We're choosing between three now, and once we know, we'll go scout it, see how hard a target it is."

I looked at Morgan. "You didn't tell them about the email."

"I did not," she said.

"Morgan." That was three, maybe a genie would appear and I could wish for a slightly more cooperative cousin.

"The email?" Luke asked at the same time. Joe, next to him, had a look on his face like, oh the email. We were emailing Annie before.

"The woman who thought we were bloggers emailed us again. This time we know she's bait. She wants to meet, to talk.

And she thinks she has the advantage," Morgan said. "Well. Silvernail thinks they have the advantage."

"Don't they?" I asked.

"Rabbits don't get trapped when they can see the snare," Morgan said.

"We're wolves." I wondered if it was too soon again for my painkillers. How long did Morgan take painkillers and everything, after she got shot? I shouldn't measure myself against her at all times, but she was what I had.

"You get my point." She sighed like I was the one being tiresome.

"So I hate to interrupt, but you've had an invitation to meet all this time, and you've been letting us do all this digging anyway?" Have I ever seen Luke so mad? I didn't think so.

"Of course I have, the last time we went into a situation without any intel, I got my cousin shot."

"You didn't—" she held up a hand almost in my face, still staring at Luke. Rich had the good grace to keep his mouth shut.

"Fair enough," he said after a long moment, and I realized just how tense I'd gotten. "Everett, how credible is this? You were part of these email hijinks to begin with, weren't you?"

"Yes, sir," Everett said. He got out his tablet. I didn't know how he let the emails drop. Or maybe he'd been checking up on it all along and keeping quiet, he'd been discreet about the baby stuff to begin with. Why did anybody do what they did? I sure didn't know. "It seems to be the same woman, I think? I mean, probably her higher-ups or somebody is using her as a mouthpiece now but looking at the back door, it's her computer that sent this anyway."

"Back door?" Luke clearly didn't think he was getting this information fast enough, but also didn't even know what questions to ask, and I'd never related to him more.

"When we first made contact with this person, and Allie and Hunter went to the clinic, she plugged a usb drive into her computer that gave me access, kinda like what we did at the other facility."

"Who else did you tell about this?" Luke looked at me, looked back at Everett. Looked at Morgan. He couldn't figure out why it would've been me. He couldn't figure out why Hunter would be involved. Was he taking it better than Rachel did? He did seem less mad.

"Rachel."

I watched Luke process this, maybe put those puzzle pieces all together. These people raised me. Fertility clinic. Weird pharmaceuticals. Their gap in intel on me. The way I wasn't really like Morgan, or anybody. Whatever his conclusion, though, he kept it to himself, and I couldn't read him at all. "I guess continue keeping it quiet," he said. "We'll re-center our concentration, see what's closest to where she wants to meet. "

"She wants it to be at the same clinic," Morgan said.

"Well you're not doing that."

"Fuck you, Luke. But also no, of course we're not doing that. I told her we were absolutely not going to the clinic. Not after what happened at the diner."

"The balls on them, at that diner," Luke said.

"I read about the diner, that was them?" Rich asked. "News said it was some kind of protest that the police had to get involved with."

"Of course it did," Everett said. "Which tells us a little more about their reach. Cops, some places. Or at least that place."

"Not like we're inclined to trust the police anyway," Morgan said, a little impatient. I couldn't figure why she was trusting Luke now, but of everybody here, Morgan was who I trusted. So she had to be right. Or at least, I had to go along with her.

"Don't the Culvers have any cop buddies?" Luke asked. He looked at Morgan, then looked at my face. "It's okay, you don't have to answer."

"No, we don't have any cop buddies, what do you even mean?" Morgan looked at me too, and all I was thinking was about how I didn't meet her 'til I had to bail her out of jail for mailbox baseball. After Rachel bailed out the rest of the people who were with her and left her overnight. "That wasn't anybody we *knew*," she said, like she could read my mind, and what she found there was just the stupidest thing.

"I didn't say anything," I protested, like I was one of those bickering little kids.

"Your face, Allie. It's always your face."

"Maybe let up a little," Luke said, I think dazed from the whiplash of Morgan blaming herself for me getting shot but also going after me every second she got.

"She's fine, she can handle it."

"Sure she can," Luke said. "But we're losing focus."

"You'll be amazed at how many things I can pay attention to at once," Morgan said, grinning. "But, I feel like we do a lotta talking about what we're going to do without getting any closer to it. And like the problem never actually goes away."

"Now what are you talking about?" I asked, out of sheer desperation. Maybe this was to buy Everett emailing time. Maybe she was just testing the waters, feeling out boundaries. Morgan was always feeling out boundaries. I really needed another painkiller and I didn't want to interrupt to ask. To bring any attention to myself, now that Luke wasn't looking at me anymore.

"You know all those locations? All those little places they got tucked away? Well what if we started going there first. Hitting those targets first. Not waiting to see what they want to try to do to us next. Corrupt their data, rob it when we can."

"You want to make this cold war a hot one," Luke said, but he didn't sound too against the idea. More like he'd been waiting for somebody to suggest something like that. Waiting for Bill to give the go-ahead on it. What did you have to do, to not be a SEAL anymore? He didn't tell us that part.

"From where I'm standing, it's already been pretty hot, my dude."

Luke started to say something, but Gina came back downstairs then. Had she been listening? No, I didn't think so. Even if I didn't know where she was, the others would have. "Rich, are we feeding five extra people tonight? Do I need to go to the store or are you?"

"Nah, it's my treat," Luke said. "It's the least we could do to repay you. What do you want? Pizza night? Do you still have that really good taco joint?"

"Thank you, Luke," Gina said, looking a little mollified. Luke really should've called ahead, but as Rich didn't seem to be the tech or military model of Ward, it was hard to say what they might've been called upon for in the past. Maybe nothing. Maybe Rich was a nurse or EMT or a butcher at the local market. "I'll let you decide. The boys will be thrilled, the way Cousin Luke always spoils them when he comes to town."

Luke shrugged. "Not too bad."

"No, not too bad. I don't have to fix any damage once you leave, thank goodness, not like your older brother." She looked at Rich again, still accusingly. "I made up the guest room for the girls, but we're going to need cots in the boys' rooms for Luke and the boys."

"I'll get them from the attic," he said. He avoided looking at Morgan's smirk, he was a quick learner.

After all that, Morgan looked at me, really looked, and then pulled a pill bottle out of her pocket. "I think we had too big a gap," she said, and handed me a painkiller.

Chapter Twenty

The kids apparently loved their Cousin Luke, and I wondered not for the first time if he was Joe and Everett's cousin too. Or Uncle. I also wondered again how old he was; he didn't seem old enough that it would be creepy if he and Morgan actually ever carried out their agreement, but he wasn't college young either. Old enough to be a Navy Seal and come home again. Old enough for Bill to seem to be treating him like second in command. Who was his older brother? Brothers? My head swam, and Morgan put me to bed until dinner, which seemed like an overreaction but I couldn't seem to make myself protest. Sleeping all day was preferable to trying to socialize with these strangers, and Luke, and the painkiller made me real comfy.

I didn't even know how many pizzas got ordered, and Rich put a leaf in their dining room table so that we all fit around it and it was more people and noise than I could stand but I also didn't want to be alone yet again in a strange house, so I grimly chewed through two slices one handed and mostly blinked at my plate.

"Why do you have that?" one of the boys asked me after all the pizza boxes were empty and getting stacked with the garbage, pointing at my sling.

"I broke my collarbone," I said.

"Does it hurt?"

I laughed a little at his big eyed expression. "Yeah, it hurts a whole lot." Unbelievably. More than anything I ever experienced before. But I knew how to be good with kids, I wasn't going to say all that.

"Zero out of ten, not recommended," Morgan said, standing up. "Have any of you ever broken a bone?"

"I had a cast for my arm!" the middle boy said. I was so tired, their names just ran out of my head like a sieve. "I had to go to school like that, and they gave me a tablet that had speech to text so I wouldn't miss any homework."

"That's right, you can't be missing homework," Gina said, looking at me like she wanted to know if I was supposed to be in school.

"Homework is important," I agreed, looking up at Morgan. I thought she seemed about at the edge of civility for the day, or maybe for her lifetime, and slowly got up as well.

"We're going to head to bed, I think," Morgan announced. "We need to get an early start in the morning."

"Do we?" Joe asked.

"Me and Allie have that errand to run," she said. "Doing it early so that we can meet back up with you down the road, in the afternoon. It's why Luke came with a different car." Was it?

"Ah yeah, let's look at a map so that we can figure out the best route for that," Luke said. He knew about the wolf, I knew he did, but maybe he didn't know about the sanctuary part.

"Sure thing," Morgan said easily. "Carry Allie's bag upstairs and we'll do that."

"My pleasure."

They went out to the Jeep while I stood at the bottom of the stairs, swaying a little. "So, I don't want it to seem like I'm keeping an eye on you," Joe said. Everett was installed on a couch and the younger boys were doling out controllers and talking about characters.

"But you are, and it's fine. I'm okay, I'm just tired," I said.

"I wish we didn't have to do any of this," he said.

"Me too." I looked at him, then past him into the room with Everett and the kids. "But if we do this, and it works, then it means nobody'll have to worry about it anymore. Those boys won't ever be afraid of what happened to my family happening to theirs."

"That's true." He wanted to say more, I think we both wanted to say more, but I heard Morgan clomping back up the front walk with Luke, smelling like fresh cigarettes. I reached out and found one of Joe's hands, gave it a squeeze. He looked at me, surprised.

"We'll be okay," I said firmly. I had to believe it, because I couldn't consider the alternative. He squeezed back, and then we dropped hands before Morgan and Luke could see, and he went to play video games with his cousins.

"You're sure just the two of you want to do this little jaunt?" Luke asked as we climbed the stairs. Morgan had me go ahead of them, I guess in case I fainted.

"Yeah, we're sure. We'll do it quick, no fuss, no muss. No sense involving more people than necessary. Plus, do you really want to see Rachel again so soon? No you do not."

"You don't sound like *you* want to see Rachel again so soon," he said, laughing.

"Our last phone conversation was a little bit fraught," she said.

"That feels like a million years ago," I said. "It was yesterday, right?"

"Yup, yesterday. See, you really do need to get some sleep."

"I slept all day," I mumbled.

The guest room had two twin beds in it, and the bathroom was right across the hall. I hadn't gotten changed this morning, but this time I took the time to get myself ready for bed. When I came back, Luke had a road map opened up on Morgan's bed and they were bent over it looking at routes, heads almost touching.

"So we'll go to where Rachel has the wolf this way. Or thereabouts," Morgan was saying. Of course she wasn't telling him where Rachel was. "And then this way to the rescue."

"Yeah, that makes sense. And then we'll meet you over here, and set up the meet that we're all sure is bait."

"It's absolutely bait," I said, getting into bed.

"See, even Allie thinks so."

"You need us to move operations?" Luke asked, looking at me appraisingly.

"No, I'm going to be out again before my head hits the pillow."

He shrugged. "If you say so."

"We'll just have to keep it down," Morgan said.

I was mostly right. I'd barely woken up enough to sit at the table and have dinner, and I drifted almost immediately. Definitely before they started talking again, but also not so deeply that I didn't hear Luke say "She isn't really operational. She shouldn't be doing any of this."

"I'm not leaving her with Rachel, if that's what you're trying to say."

"That's exactly what I'm trying to say. Why not?"

"The wolf is hers, as a for-instance."

"And what else, those people? The ones she said raised her."

"There's just some things you need to do yourself, whether you're at one hundred percent or not." Like getting Rachel out of that facility, with or without Ward help, I thought. Or maybe I was just dreaming this. "Allie says she's doing it, and I'm going to let her do it. We couldn't stop her the other time she took it in her head to go ramming off."

"I'm concerned she's a liability," Luke said.

"We're all liabilities," Morgan said, and that was when I fell asleep for real.

It wasn't an easy sleep, but it was a deep one. I sometimes shifted and the pain woke me up part of the way, but I didn't wake up enough to have to get up in the night.

I opened my eyes at dawn, feeling out of touch but no longer exhausted; the house was quiet, and Morgan was sleep-breathing in the bed next to me, and I was happy to just lay there and wait for the day to find us.

Somebody went down to the kitchen and got coffee started, but there was too much going on, smell-wise, and I couldn't decide who I thought it was. Morgan made a noise and rolled over, then sat up. "I feel like I overslept," she said.

"What, and missed the big exam?"

"Silly Allie, I never went to *school*." She swung her feet to the floor, stood up and stretched.

"Then I don't know what else you could've overslept for and missed."

"There's plenty of things. Like a flight for a tour." She shook her hair out in front of the mirror, bundled it back again into a ponytail. "You need help getting ready?"

"No. I don't know. Just my hair I guess." I sat up, and she did my ponytail too, a little too tight but I wasn't going to complain.

"Meet me in the kitchen, then. We'll see how Joe's coffee is."

I probably should've let her help me. I was more like Morgan at times than I realized, stubbornly doing things on my own that I had no business doing, and if she could tell that it was Joe in the kitchen making coffee, she could definitely tell that I was sweaty and panting by the time I changed my clothes, and that I dabbed away some blood with toilet paper before flushing away that evidence. But for us, or for me, fresh blood smell always seemed to hang in the air for a long time. It was like how it was impossible to get rid of glitter. It was why I couldn't smell that Morgan had been shot that night, because there was already so much blood, so much going on, saturating my newfound senses.

By the time I made it to the kitchen, Everett was there too, head and shoulders into the fridge. Years of Mama telling me to tie my shoes, I was going to break my neck, made me real uncomfortable walking around with my boots untied, but it couldn't be helped. I wasn't going to ask anybody to tie my boots for me. "I thought we ate all the pizza," he said, coming up with triangular-shaped foil packaging.

"You just thought that because Gina actually puts food away," Joe said, glancing at me as I came in the door.

"I didn't think there was food to put away. That doesn't happen at home very often."

"You two are up early," I said. Morgan sat at the table with a mug of coffee in front of her, texting and frowning.

"Luke likes getting an early start," Joe said. I looked around. "He's packing the truck."

"Oh." I didn't really know what-all Luke had to pack in the truck. Maybe he'd had things here that Rich was holding onto for him. It wasn't really my business. I poured a cup of coffee and sat at the table across from Morgan, who flicked her eyes up at me for a second, but then her phone vibrated again. "Tell Hunter I say hi."

"Sure thing."

"Has she had a hard time over any of this?" Everett asked. "From her sister or anything?"

"Not that she's said." It was impossible to tell if Morgan was telling the truth or if she was just irritated at the question. I raised my eyebrows and sipped the coffee. Hunter was like Morgan; what outside consequences could possibly have an effect on her actions? "Other than losing her car."

"Oh I didn't even think of that," I said, and Morgan glanced up at me again, squinted a little, like she was asking a question, but I didn't begin to understand.

The front door closed and Luke came down the hall. "Come on, you two, I'd rather get out of here before Gina martyrs herself on making us breakfast or something. Eggs taste better without all the family drama, we'll stop on the road." He came into the kitchen and stopped, looked at me and Morgan, who'd chosen that moment to finish her coffee. "Morning."

"Morning," I said after too long a pause. I'd expected him to say 'morning *ladies*' and he didn't, and I didn't know what changed.

"Everybody doing okay?" He didn't look at me in particular, but we all knew he meant me. A liability, I thought. He thought.

"Just peachy," Morgan said, scraping her chair back and dropping her phone in her pocket. "You ready, Allie?"

"Oh I left my bag in…" she just looked at me, and I drank the rest of my coffee and put the mug in the sink. She let the screen door slam behind her. "I'll get it and be right down."

"Do you want me to?" Joe asked.

"No, it's okay." Maybe that was it, Morgan just wanted to put me in a position to lie over and over again, until it fit like a worn-in shirt. "Thanks, though, I appreciate it."

"What a pair you are. She always so fucking sunny in the morning?" Luke asked.

"Aw, Morgan's sunny all the time, if you know how to look at it." I grinned, hard, and he laughed.

"Sure she is. You two be careful."

"Always are." Weird that saying that didn't feel like lying. I ducked out of the kitchen while he was still chuckling and shaking his head.

The kids all seemed to still be asleep, but I could hear Gina and Rich talking in low voices in their room, and I tried to be extra quiet getting my bag. It was hard, in an unfamiliar house, all the squeaks that I didn't know. But they had the good grace to ignore me and stay in their room. I couldn't see taking the time to try and make the beds one-handed, Morgan was liable to just start leaning on the horn out front, but I did make a gesture at pulling the comforters up. The room still smelled a lot like Luke, too; I wondered how long he stayed talking to Morgan after I dropped off. Maybe he told her SEAL stories and she told him rock star stories.

I grabbed my bag and went downstairs, and when I glanced up the hall, Joe waved to me from the kitchen door and I found a smile for him.

Chapter Twenty-One

"They know we're coming, right?" I asked as Morgan made what I thought was the final turn, though she'd made what I thought was the final turn about four times already.

"They knew we would be, once we heard from the sanctuary. You told Rachel you were doing that."

"Yeah, but—" She turned her face towards me for just a second, looking at me straight on through her sunglasses, and then turned back to the road. "Just seems like a bad idea to surprise them. Especially now."

"I don't disagree, but it'll be fine," she said.

"They'll recognize the jeep," I said, wishing I hadn't asked to begin with.

"You got there." She smirked.

"All by myself." I looked out the window; we got off the highway a long time ago, taking two-laned county routes that wound through hills and fields, passed falling-down barns and cow fields, and the occasional two-blocks of a Main Street of a town where three of the seven houses would be on sale, but they still had a church, and a fire department, and a brick post office. The sun was out and the weather was beautiful and Morgan pushed the speed limit the way she always did, but it was the kind of day when, despite everything that happened and was still happening, it seemed like everything was perfect and nothing bad could possibly happen.

Finally, though, we turned off the county road onto an unpainted, cracked blacktop, went past two driveways, and then turned onto two ruts that went through some trees, and to a dip in between some more hills, and there was the latest Culver hideout. I didn't know who kept track of them all, or how. I didn't know if they were all still owned and paid for. They seemed to be, the ones I'd been to so far.

Rachel was standing on the top of the porch steps by the time we parked and got out, the dogs circling around her. We came across the dooryard and she came off the steps and caught Morgan up in a strong, tight hug, so suddenly that Morgan made a funny little noise as the air whiffed out of her. They stood like that for a minute, Morgan's arms trapped against her sides, her hands flexing, livewire tension across her shoulders and down her back.

Then she let go and said "Come here, Allie," in a tear-roughened voice. She wasn't crying, exactly, but her eyes had the shimmer. I did, and I *was* crying, and she hugged me too, but not so tight, taking care of my shoulder. I could feel Morgan standing off awkwardly behind us.

Sela came outside. "Oh thank goodness," she said, and I heard Morgan's short sniff and thought oh no, this wasn't the homecoming that the aunts thought it was. Oh no.

Rachel let me go, and Morgan was crouched to Dio, roughing up his ears and neck, smiling hard. We wouldn't be doing this if it weren't for me, I thought. If I hadn't taken that wolf out of Silvernail when we took Rachel out.

"That was some stunt you pulled," Rachel said to me, standing back a little now, looking both me and Morgan up and down.

"I didn't think I'd be able to," I admitted. My fault, this was my fault. Or it was Mama's fault but I'd made it worse. "I thought for sure somebody would stop me before I even got out of the door."

"Well you did. Scared us half to death," Sela said. She hugged me too, even more gently still, seeming to be well aware of what hurt where. "I'm so glad you're alright. We're so happy to see you. We're so happy you're—"

"We got the wolf a place at a sanctuary," I said in a rush. I couldn't stand it anymore "We're here for him."

Sela looked at me a second longer, still smiling, before her face fell. And it was like a door slammed in Rachel's eyes, and she turned to Morgan, who'd straightened up again. "You're not staying." She wasn't asking. Sidney came silently out onto the porch, her eyes big.

"No, Mama," Morgan said quietly and her tone froze my tears.

"You can't possibly *trust*—"

"We *don't*!" Morgan balled her fists, and Dio's hair ruffled across his shoulders. "But they're seeing it as their own interests right now, and it's something we gotta see through. It's something Allie has to see through."

"Alleluia is that true?" Rachel asks, crushing me with her regard.

"Yes ma'am," I said, licking my lips. She looked at me for a long minute, maybe a few minutes, maybe thinking of the 'stunt' I pulled. Maybe thinking of whatever hopes she'd had for Morgan. For Dulcie. For me.

"Okay then," Rachel said in the most colorless tone of voice I'd ever heard. "Get the wolf, and get on out of here."

"We'll be back after we—" Morgan started, and Rachel stopped her.

"No, daughter mine. You won't."

Sela said "Rachel, no" ever so softly, and a muscle in Rachel's jaw twitched.

"Rachel, I—"

"No, Morgan, I don't have any other way to get through to you, and I don't have any other way to keep this family safe. When you leave here, we're going to go to ground. Again. Further. And those people won't be able to find us anymore, and do this to us ever again. It's the only way that we can protect ourselves, against people like that. With money like that. We can't win a war."

"The Wards are helping us. And maybe more families will get involved."

"You just said that you didn't trust them, why would you use that as a defense?"

"But Rachel, they really are," I said, and she dismissed me with a glance.

"Where's the wolf sanctuary?" she asked. "How far from here?"

"Couple hours," Morgan said, confused.

"Take the wolf. If you don't come back after that, then don't come back."

"Rachel," Sela said.

"Sela, go in the house." Rachel's tone was clear and even, not barbed, and not to be questioned. Sela gave me another quick hug, a little rougher this time, and my breath caught in my throat. I saw Rachel take note. "Does that sound fair? Morgan? Allie?"

"No," I choked out. Morgan didn't say anything, just stared with burning eyes.

"Let me try again. Do you *understand*?"

"We understand," Morgan said grimly.

"Thank you. Best get to it then."

We stood there a moment, not moving. If I never moved again, I thought, then nothing would get worse. Though also nothing could ever get better again. Sela and Sidney were back inside, out of sight. "Where is he?"

"Around back. His equipment's on the back porch."

I went behind the house. The enclosure wasn't an acre, but it was bigger than a normal dog run anyway. John Doe was standing right up against the fence, his eyes locking on me the second I was in view. He could sense the tension in the air, in our voices, and me, and he was tense too, ears forward, holding himself rigid and light. "Sorry it's been a while," I said to him. "I'm gonna come in and get you harnessed up, and then we're going in the car. I'm taking you someplace where you can be safe and do all the living you need to do, within reason. You won't be shut up and bored in little spaces like this anymore. I tried really hard, they'll do better. They know what they're doing." He flicked his ears, and I wondered how much he understood. But he didn't rush the gate when I opened it, and stood to be harnessed about how he had every other time.

I clipped the leash on, and took a deep breath to steady myself before I could go face Rachel again. And Morgan. Lord knew she and Rachel butted heads a lot, but this was past a line that I don't think either of us knew existed. I didn't see how Rachel could mean it, but I believed her that she meant it.

They were both standing in the same places when I came back out front with the wolf. I didn't hear them say anything the entire time I was out of sight, and even now, Morgan kind of quirked her lips and stalked back to the jeep. Dio followed along behind her, and jumped up into the back when she put her hand on the door. Her eyes got big the way Sidney's had been.

After a second, some internal struggle, she said, "Oh Dio...no bud, you gotta stay here." He flattened his ears and looked at her.

"Morgan, I could ride in back with the wolf and Dio can ride up front." I wasn't sure I could take this, after everything else. "We can make it work."

"We can't bring him," she said with a ragged edge in her voice. She'd left him with the neighbor before, when the house in the pines burned. The Wards didn't have dogs at any of their alphabet camps. Wolves didn't bring dogs to war. "Dio. Out." She reached for his collar and he flattened against the seat, scooting back away from her.

John Doe sighed, and I looked at Rachel, who stood and watched with her arms folded. He was Morgan's dog, he wouldn't listen to me. Morgan pulled the driver door open and folded her seat forward against the steering wheel, stepping up on the running board and gritting her teeth as she reached for him again. He stood up to spin around, maybe to jump in the cargo area, and she caught his collar and pulled him against her, pressing her face against his for a moment. "I'm so fucking sorry," she said, just for Dio, but of course me and Rachel could hear. Then she lifted him up and hopped down out of the Jeep, grunting as she landed, and walked past Rachel with her wriggling dog in her arms. I stood there for a second, listening to her march back around the house the way I came, and put him in the enclosure I'd just taken the wolf out of.

John Doe pulled on the leash then, and I let him jump into the Jeep. I looked at Rachel, not knowing what to say, how to say goodbye. From the look on her face, she didn't either. Morgan came back, and Dio let out the most unearthly wail as she limped past Rachel to the Jeep and slammed the driver's seat back into place, swung up into it. She jammed her sunglasses on, and started the engine. There just wasn't anything to say. I got into the passenger seat and Morgan pulled away before I had my seatbelt settled, kicking up a rooster tail of dust behind us as we drove.

Chapter Twenty-Two

With the top down on the Jeep, John Doe sat up in the middle of the backseat, his nose tipped up into the wind. I turned around to look at him periodically. He was beautifully handsome, and I was absolutely not the right person to be keeping him. Really, nobody in the world should be keeping him, he should just be able to be out in the world and existing. But at this point, he had no fear of man, and even a sort of contempt for people that worried me. The sanctuary was the best. I'd already decided on that, of course, but I still felt awful about it. Like I failed him somehow. He would be happy there, I thought. He would be with other wolves like him, as opposed to wolves like us.

And I just couldn't stop crying. For him, for us. For all of us.

Morgan was Morgan, of course. The tape deck was blasting, louder than normal even, but she wasn't singing along. She was gripping the steering wheel tight enough that her knuckles were pale, scars on them standing out. The mostly healed scuffs from when she punched Luke Ward were stark in the sunlight. I wished I could say something, to comfort her, to comfort me; this was the second time in my life that I was given a very clear 'and don't come back' kind of farewell, and I hadn't expected it either time. This one hurt even worse. Rachel knew us, she understood us.

She glared at me if I sniffled, and I mopped my face with a bandanna and tried to keep it to myself. We were doing the right thing. Rachel had to see that. Rachel had to change her mind, and once we were done, we'd find them and be a family. Whatever that meant for us. It would be okay, it had to be okay.

We stopped for gas at one point, Morgan wordlessly hopping out to go into the convenience store while I took John Doe off to a meager grassed area to see if he had to pee or anything. He sniffed around intently and I was nervous, so scared, that he was going to just break and run, get away from me, and we'd lose him forever on the highway. He was smart enough to avoid cars, but he'd be hunted down and shot, I was certain. If he got loose. But he didn't get loose. We got back in the car right as Morgan came out, and she unwrapped a hotdog and handed it back to him, as though he was just another dog on a road trip, getting people food as a treat. He took it from her with surprising delicacy.

We drove past the entryway two different times, and then finally made the right turn. John Doe stood up on the back seat, sniffing audibly, his nostrils flared and his ears swiveling this and that. He was tense and ready, and so very interested. He could smell them, and then I could smell them. The other wolves that were here. There was dense brush, and there were lots of trees, and when I looked I could see the fences, all of the fences. Morgan eased up the long lane, practically a road unto itself, that then turned into a driveway in front of a big lodge. I think I remembered from the website that people could come and camp here, take classes to educate themselves on wolves. It was ridiculous, it was funny, for Morgan and I to be here. Not so much for what I could tell people about wolves, but I'm sure Morgan had that level of insight. But I still felt like a wolf in sheep's clothing as we got out of the Jeep and the woman who had emailed me came out of the lodge to meet us.

"You must be Allie," she said, and started to hold out her hand but then looked at my sling. "Are you all right?"

"Camping accident," I said, the lie out of my mouth before I could even think about it. Maybe Morgan's lie therapy was working. "Not a big deal. Not related to him."

"He's a nice looking one," she said, peering past us and into the back of the Jeep. John Doe still stood on the backseat, looking at me intently. "You've taken good care of him."

"I tried really hard," I said, tearing up again in spite of myself. "He's just too much for me, though, and I really want him to be as happy as he can be, and as free as he can be." I wanted that for all of us.

"That's what we want for the wolves here as well," the woman said, smiling. She must have dealt with people crying all the time, thank God, my emotional regulation wasn't going to be a problem for once. "Do you want to get him out of the Jeep? We've handled the paperwork already. There's a separate area over here where we put the newcomers, where they can still see and smell the others, while everybody acclimates to one another and decompresses."

"And does that work?" Morgan asked, in a tone almost of professional curiosity. She was still wearing her sunglasses.

"It does, actually. We don't have what would be considered a pack exactly, because it isn't like they're here voluntarily. They aren't a family unit, they can't leave if it isn't working out. But we've got a big enough property where occasionally the more juvenile members can kind of split off and do their own thing, if they find socially that works out better for them. And where we can keep the individuals separate who can't or won't get along."

"So they never fight?" I looked at Morgan's hands, but the woman didn't know to do that, and still kept on smiling.

"They don't ever get to that point, no. If we notice tensions, we go in and shuffle them around, break up the tensions, and that's worked out very well for us all so far."

"That's good, that's great," I said.

"So just like that, we're just gonna turn him loose?" Morgan asked.

"Just like that," she said, but she was looking at me now too. John Doe hadn't dropped his gaze. "No sense drawing it out, right? And of course you can come back and visit if you'd like, the same as everybody else. If you feel like that's something you might want to do."

"I might," I said. "I don't know." Never. I would never. It wouldn't do either of us any good.

"Also, of course, once you do this there's no taking him back."

"I know that. This is the best thing for him."

"Good then." She smiled, and then she stood back. Morgan did too, and I didn't know if I was thankful for that or if I was mad at her for not doing this for me. But nobody could do this for me, and nobody was ever going to do this for me. I had to do it for myself.

I went back to the Jeep and pulled open the door, leaned my seat forward so I could reach in and unsnap the seatbelt harness. I had the leash firmly in hand before John Doe looked at me and decided it was time to hop out. He stood next to me as though we'd trained and were comfortable with one another, just looking around and looking up at me occasionally, and the livewire smell of his interest and excitement was almost all

I *could* smell. But he was happy, too. Calmly excited, if such a thing existed. I guess it had to.

We walked over to Morgan and the woman, who looked very surprised. "He's a very good boy, isn't he," she said.

I smiled tightly, not quite true, and nodded. "He sure is. He does his best." He was who he was, I thought. It wasn't his job to be a good boy, like a dog. If I'd ever thought wolves and dogs were about the same, by this point I knew without question that it wasn't true at all. They were like one another, yes, but not the same at all, not anymore. Wolves were wolves and dogs were dogs. The woman gestured, and I followed her with John Doe, Morgan trailing behind, like she was still interested in spite of herself. Like she didn't have anything better going on, so she might as well tag along.

We passed through the lodge, where other sanctuary employees worked here and there, but nobody intercepted us. There were no other wolves visible, but I didn't expect there to be. I could smell them, though, and once or twice heard them distantly. They could smell him too, they were curious, but holding themselves at a remove, even further than the fences would. I had to wonder how much it shook them up, or didn't, every time a new addition came in. Normal wolves were shy, unlike the rest of us. I had to wonder what they thought of smelling us, wolves like people, and how that might affect his reception. What they could ask him, what he could tell them.

When we were outside behind the lodge, the property just seemed to go on and on, and we walked for a little while, through a couple of different gates. Still no visible wolves. Still some curious wolf sounds. Morgan tilted her head occasionally, and was smiling, but she didn't say anything. It was a dangerous thing, sometimes, when Morgan didn't say anything, especially after the day we'd had. Especially with what our near future promised. But the grass and the trees were all so very green it was almost like all the colors were turned up for spring, not a whole lot of flowering things here, but some, and the sky was big and blue and almost cloudless, just a few wisps. The air was crisp and clean, and I tilted my head back for an appreciative sniff myself, unable to help it. It was beautiful here and I hoped John Doe could be happy.

Then we got to the last gate, and the woman unlocked it and motioned me in with John Doe. "I'll let you go on ahead. Say your goodbyes, and turn him loose. You don't need me in there for that."

"I'll wait out here too," Morgan said, probably because it would've been weird for her to keep not saying anything.

John Doe and I walked through the gate and the woman closed it behind us. He looked up at me expectantly as we walked a little ways into the enclosure. Not really an enclosure, it wasn't like the box I'd tried to keep him in, because it was all I had. Inside the fence, it was like forest and wilderness. I didn't know how far we would have to walk to find the other fence, to make out the boundaries of this particular enclosure. So much better than I could do for him anywhere else. I put my hand on his back, felt his smooth rough hair spring up through my fingers one last time. I didn't want to cry again, keep crying again. It wouldn't change anything, wouldn't change my mind even. It wouldn't change Rachel's mind. But John Doe was one of the first decisions I'd made all on my own as a wolf, and letting him go was one of the hardest decisions I'd made in either of my lives.

Then I reached down and unbuckled the leash from his harness, letting it hang on just his collar. The harness snaps fell away easily and he stepped out of the webbing, looking up and away from me, his nose twitching again, his tail at half-mast straight out behind him. He wanted to run. He wanted to be free. I stroked his neck once, and then slipped the end of his collar out of its loop, pulled the tongue loose, tag rattling in my hands. And then he was free, no leash no collar or harness, nothing. Just a wolf standing in his new wilderness. He shook himself off, as though he'd suddenly gotten wet, and he reached up and swiped my hand with his tongue a single time. I watched him walk off slowly, looking at the trees, sniffing the grass, sniffing the air again. He was almost to the underbrush, almost out of sight, when he turned and looked at me, locking eyes. Then he turned and was gone.

Sometimes you said I love you by letting go.

Acknowledgements

Thank you to Jim for your love and support.

Thank you to Premee, or your WARWLF enthusiasm!

Thank you to Lennon, for proofreading, and being there. I've really valued our friendship over the years!

Thank you to my Eternal Gratitude patrons, Brian, Sheryl, Wendy, Kelly, and Heather, I appreciate that you believe in me, and your commitment to my writing!

And thanks to all my new readers, who heard that these weren't like other werewolves, and are now two books deep with me!

Jennifer R. Donohue grew up at the Jersey Shore and now lives in central New York with her husband and their Dobermans. She works at her local public library where she also facilitates a writing workshop. Her work has appeared in *Apex Magazine*, *Escape Pod*, *Fusion Fragment*, and elsewhere. Her Run With the Hunted novella series is available in paperback and ebook, and her debut novel, Exit Ghost, is available in ebook and hardcover. She tweets @AuthorizedMusin and you can subscribe to her Patreon for a new short story every month:https://www.patreon.com/JenniferRDonohue

Other Works by Jennifer R. Donohue:
Exit Ghost

• • • •

The Drowned Heir

• • • •

Learn to Howl

• • • •

Run With the Hunted (series)
Run With the Hunted
Run With the Hunted 2: Ctrl Alt Delete
Run With the Hunted 3: Standard Operating Procedure
Run With the Hunted 4: VIP
Run With the Hunted 5: Insert Coin to Play
Run With the Hunted 6: Burned Asset